SOMEWHERE IN BETWEEN

BY Katie Li

KUNG-FU GIRL
BOOKS

Boston, Massachusetts

Edited by Tanya Gold
Book design and text production by Colleen Cole

Cover photograph: Dahlia Farm © by Alexander Byron Balogh, Portland Oregon; digitally composited with illustration of roller coaster corkscrew © by Colleen Cole. Interior photography: Ivy © by Colleen Cole; Rose © by Katie Li. Kung Fu Girl Books logo by Ashley Parkin.

Kung Fu Girl Books
P.O. Box 301373
Boston, MA 02130
www.kungfugirlbooks.com

FIRST EDITION

Library of Congress Cataloging-in-Publication Data has been applied for.

ISBN: 978-0-9966020-0-6

For Kyle

TUESDAY IS ALWAYS THE WORST day. Worse than Monday. You know Monday will be bad. From the moment the dismissal bell rings on Friday afternoon, each hour is one less hour of freedom, one hour closer to that moment when you open your eyes on Monday morning and wish you'd never woken up."

"And you think Tuesday is worse than *that*?" Rom asked, keeping pace with Magnolia as she trudged through the park in her combat boots.

"Yes," she said. "Because you expect Monday to suck. But Tuesday? There's nothing special about Tuesday, not even the distinction of being the worst. It's the most excruciatingly normal day of the week."

"So, Friday is the best day."

"No, Thursday is the best day."

Over the past few weeks since they'd started walking home together, Rom had begun to understand her ticks and rhythms. At least he thought he did. And then she would say something unexpected and he would have to construct his idea of her all over again.

"Why is Thursday the best day?"

"Because Thursday you have the anticipation of Friday—so many things could happen, the possibilities are endless on Thursday. But when Friday comes you have to actually start living them out and they're never as good as you were hoping."

She sounded sad, and he thought it might have something to do with Zane, who they didn't usually talk about. Rom could tell it wasn't a coincidence that she started hanging out with him after Zane stopped hanging out with her.

"And when Friday comes you have to start the countdown to Monday," she added.

"So, the anticipation that makes Thursday the best is the same anticipation that makes Monday—or Tuesday—the worst."

She looked up at him, not smiling, but bright-eyed and pleased. "Yeah—I hadn't thought of it that way. But that's exactly it."

Rom wanted to ask her then, *Maybe we could do something fun on Friday?* The words were formed in his mouth, but his heart was beating so hard he was afraid he'd mess it up. She had only just started talking to him, even though they had been in the same homeroom since she arrived as a transfer student last year.

She'd maintained an even, penetrating gaze as she stood by the blackboard when their teacher introduced her to the class. She'd worn the standard gray uniform like everyone else. But her hair, which had an uneven texture—a mix of tight and loose curls—was dyed in varying shades of pink and purple and red. He had been too intimidated to approach her, and even now was careful as he phrased things, not wanting to sound lame. After learning her sentiments about Fridays, he figured that he would only disappoint her.

His question remained unspoken and dissolved with a couple exhales.

She wasn't the only punk at school, but there was something about Magnolia that made her special. It was the way her shoulder blades protruded through her shirt, like budding wings, the small gauges in her ears that caught a tiny bit of sunlight. He studied her hair when he should have been paying attention to the lecture or the classwork, and would contemplate what it reminded him of.

Her hair, he decided, was like a sunset.

Except now it was dyed blue.

It was the start of their junior year, and already their teachers and parents were bearing down on them with questions about college. Every day they returned home and there was suddenly a pile of glossy postcards and brochures from universities that all looked the same. The same official-looking emblems, the same stock photos of kids leaning over bunsen burners or playing the cello or groups of smiling "friends" looking wholesome and happy to be in college and learning stuff.

They used to not get any mail at all.

"What schools are you going to apply to?" their classmates asked. "What are you going to major in?"

Magnolia didn't know how everyone already had their answers. She knew she was smart, and had always wanted to go to college, but she never knew what she wanted to be when she grew up. She thought that was something people just figured out as they went along. Except she had been going along, and nothing was figured out.

Talking to Zane seemed like an obvious path to a solution. But he'd told her he was too busy to make time for her anymore.

She didn't want to talk about Zane, the same way she didn't want to think about going to college.

Magnolia and Rom found plenty of other things to talk about during their long walks home from school—utopia, the nature of time, lucid dreaming, or the best texture of chocolate chip cookies. He preferred them more wafer-like and crisp, while she liked them dense and chewy.

Their banter came easy, but they didn't spend time together past their walks. They didn't meet up on the weekends, or hang out during school. She was too busy teaching herself things that were more interesting than whatever lessons their teachers had prepared, and he was too busy just trying to keep his grades up. All they had were their walks through the park, under shadows that were disappearing as the autumn leaves continued to fall.

Maybe because it was the last warm day, they walked a little slower. They found reasons to pause—to fix an undone shoelace or examine bark on a tree—or they would stop entirely for dramatic effect as they waxed poetic. They both knew that, once winter arrived, their afternoon walks would come to an end.

And that's when they found the in-between place.

They stood at the train station where they usually said good-bye. Evening commuters spilled into the street and dispersed—some up the hill to the fancy old mansions, others across the footbridge to the low-rise apartment buildings and run-down houses. Magnolia and Rom would have to leave each other for their own separate worlds.

"Hey—" She looked at something over his shoulder. "Have you ever noticed that gate before?"

Past the station was an iron gate, slightly open. Magnolia had passed through this station for years, but this was the first time she'd seen the gate.

Something about it, the way it was left ajar, was like an invitation.

FIVE YEARS LATER, MAGNOLIA wakes up on the floor.

There's a thin, less-than-a-moment when she feels normal, but then looking at the dust bunnies under the radiator reminds her that she is back at her mother's house, in her old room in the attic, that her bed is gone, and so is Zane.

She tosses her sweat-soaked pillow aside and stares up at the skylight above the futon. How many hours of her life had she spent gazing up at this square of sky? Before she left for college, she had lain here for as long as she could because she thought she would never come back. After they loaded up the car, she held back tears as she watched her neighborhood turn into open highway behind them. She didn't want to cry in front of her mother.

It was stupid of her to think that she would be gone forever. Now that she's back, like the slide down to start in Snakes and Ladders, it's like college never happened. Nothing ever changed.

Her room is the same. Same slanted ceilings with posters and murals she painted on the walls. Landscapes inspired by her trips with Rom to the in-between place—run-down buildings and scorched earth and psychedelic clouds. Her mom once came up to the attic, looked at the murals, and asked her, "Is everything okay?" followed by, "Have you been taking drugs?"

Magnolia never took drugs. Maybe she would have if her boyfriend hadn't been a dealer, but as it was, she had no interest.

She glances over at her shelves lined with trinkets she picked up off the sidewalk, or found in the in-between place. Books and mixed CDs. An empty round mint tin filled with paper stars. Vases of dead roses. Small stuffed animals. A broken rubik's cube. Blue sea glass. A delicate pink flower. Love letters and phone numbers written on bar napkins. Shoe boxes of objects that she used to carry in her bag—can openers, highlighters, note cards, stickers, fortunes plucked from uneaten cookies, cut-out horoscopes, a mini bible, pez dispensers. Junk jewelry that never adorned her fingers.

Sometimes, she brought home bigger things. A panel of stained glass that she had pulled from someone's yard on trash day. An overstuffed chair left on the curb that was so heavy she'd had to drag it, losing one of its stumpy wooden legs in the process. She'd propped it back up with a stack of hardcover tomes the library was giving away. She had taken them, knowing that she would never read them. And yet, they still found some purpose. That's how it went with all her lost and found objects.

But now she doesn't care anymore. She spends her days on the little balcony outside her bedroom, looking out at the backyard. She used to have this fantasy of growing flowers or herbs in mismatched pots out there. But now it's cluttered with empty beer bottles and rotting lime and a ceramic bowl she had been using as an ashtray. Now she lies on the futon with her feet on the wall, looking up at the clouds. She had taken the bed with her when she and Zane moved in together after college. She never brought it back.

It's hard to believe that was only a year ago.

She hadn't realized how much could happen in a single year.

Now she wakes up each morning with the sun shining into her face, and she wonders how it manages, day after day, year after year, to move across the sky—not caring, not stopping.

Its relentless consistency mocks her inability to do simple things like make lunch or fall asleep at night. She tries reading, but can never focus on the words. She never remembers when she fell asleep but wakes up every morning with the sun shining through her skylight. She refuses to move the futon out of its path. She belongs here as much as the sun.

She fights the sun every day even though she knows it's a battle she'll never win.

Most mornings, Magnolia comes down the creaky attic steps to an empty house. By then, her mother is gone and the rooms are sunlit and silent. She can go to the bathroom and brush her teeth, the toilet still running while she stands at the sink. She can go to the kitchen and take an oversized mug from the cupboard and fill it with ice and cooled coffee her mother brewed hours earlier. She can return to her room in the attic—unnoticed and undisturbed—to waste the day.

But today, she steps into the hall and hears faint static. The almost-silent electric buzz leaves her feeling off-balance. Then she realizes that it must mean her mother is home.

"Mom?" Her voice sounds clunky and awkward, because she doesn't talk much anymore.

"Good morning," her mother calls from her bedroom.

Magnolia approaches the doorway and sees her mother sitting on her already made bed, the newspaper spread across her bright floral quilt. She's reading a section while watching the news.

"Don't you have work?" Magnolia stands in the hall, not wanting to get too close. Her mom might wave her in and they'd spend the morning watching talk shows and soap operas.

That's one of her mom's tactics to get her to talk about what happened to Zane.

Magnolia doesn't like being around when her mom is home. Her mom tiptoes around her with pity, trying to take care of her, offering her reassurance that feels inappropriate.

There are other fish in the sea.

Don't worry—you're young, you still have time.

Sometimes her mother recounts Zane's good qualities. *So smart, so charming.* Or she talks about what happened. *Such a tragedy. There was so much hope in his future.* Magnolia knows her mother thought they would get married, someday. Magnolia once thought that, too—which is crazy, in retrospect.

You don't marry drug dealers.

She knows that her mom loved Zane. Everyone loved Zane. He was a manipulator, he had everyone thinking one thing, but in truth, he was actually the opposite. Now that he's gone, everyone has made him a martyr. Really, Magnolia knows, he was a monster.

"Can't I take the day off to spend some time with my daughter?" her mom asks. "I thought we could go to the furniture store and get you a new bed."

"Oh—" That's the last thing Magnolia wants to do. "I actually have some plans today."

Magnolia tries not to flush or stammer at her lie.

"That's okay." Her mom brightens. Magnolia can tell her mother has been worried about her, the way she holes herself up in the attic, barely coming down, never changing her clothes. "Maybe this weekend?"

"Maybe," Magnolia replies, closing the bathroom door behind her.

Her mother at home puts a damper on her plans of chain-smoking and staring out the window, doing nothing. That's all she wants to do. Nothing. Magnolia can see the circles under her eyes and the dullness of her skin. She can't deny that she is depressed—and has been for a long time.

She's too depressed to care about fixing her depression.

It's strange to be outside.

Magnolia had been out on her balcony, but the balcony is different from being in public. She stands with her toes on the edge of the front porch and looks out at the street like she's getting ready to jump from a high diving board into a pool. Or off a cliff.

She wonders where is she going to go, what she is going to do.

She doesn't want to see anyone. She doesn't want to run into anyone who might know her. She doesn't want to talk about what happened. She doesn't want to be seen. If only she could just be invisible, stepping off the porch and walking down the street without needing to stand awkwardly at the corner, waiting for the light to turn red.

She scans the street for something familiar, but the neighborhood has changed in the last five years. She had been using home as a layover between semesters, not noticing how the corner store where she used to get push-pops or ice cream sandwiches was gone, replaced by a cafe. Across the street is a new building with a doggy daycare. The nursing home was sold to a developer who is turning it into condos.

She wonders who could even afford these places. Not the kids who grew up here. They've all moved farther outside the city to cheaper towns.

Her mother used to remind her that, even though they didn't have much, at least they had the house.

Magnolia knows how hard her mother works—long, late hours at the hospital. It's rare for her mother to return home without a story about something heartbreaking or horrifying that happened in the emergency room. Even though they own the house, it's wrought with problems that her mother doesn't know how to fix—or have enough money to pay someone else to fix them.

Magnolia had replaced the grout between the pink tiles in the bathroom and patched the broken window screens. She had painted the porch creamy off-white, learning the not-so-subtle difference between high gloss and semi-gloss. She had even painted the whole house by herself, the summer after she started high school. Her mom had asked if they should paint it a new color. But Magnolia was happy with the same country blue.

Her mother tends to the garden in her free time, growing flowers in beds and up a trellis along the side of the house. Roses bloom through the chain-link fence. They live on a busy street with lots of pedestrians, and people toss their litter over the fence into her mother's garden. Magnolia used to go into a rage over this, sometimes even chasing people down to throw their garbage back at them. But her mother rarely got angry. She'd remind Magnolia that people are all just doing their best.

She said this even as she picked old baggies of dog waste out of her vegetable patch.

Magnolia has never understood how her mother could be so forgiving. But she knows that quality makes her mom an exceptional nurse.

She doesn't want her mother to worry, so she has to leave the house. All the time spent alone in the attic leaves her feeling unsure of what is real anymore. She knows that this is her home and always has been, but doesn't recognize the street or the people—the new moms pushing baby carriages or young couples walking their dogs. They walk with an assurance that she doesn't feel anymore, like they've always been here, like they were never scared.

Magnolia knows that she's changed as much as this place—not necessarily for the better—and it all happened behind her back, while she wasn't paying attention.

She steps off the porch.

When Rom comes home from college, his room is gone.

He arrives at his father's house with his girlfriend, Elyse. He takes her by the hand—dropping their suitcases on the foyer's cool white marble floor—and leads her into the corridor under the grand staircase to the basement door. They follow the twisting stairs down. He stops at the bottom.

The carpet had been torn out, replaced with lacquered hardwood floors. The dividing wall that was covered in movie posters had been knocked down to make way for an open-concept floor plan. No more drum kit. No more wall mounted shelves of board games and fantasy paperbacks and figurines. His record player and vinyl collection are missing.

Elyse surveys this new in-law apartment, admiring the furniture and installed fireplace and the kitchenette with Scandinavian cabinets, while Rom sits on the steps in a state of shock.

"Don't be sad, Rom," she says. "This place looks awesome."

He doesn't have anything to say.

"Besides, I'm sure this is a way sexier bachelor pad than however your room was before."

Then Rom really doesn't have anything to say. He just reaches up to hug her waist and she wraps her arms around him, too.

They have a week together before Elyse leaves for a volunteer job abroad. Neither one of them like the idea of a long distance relationship. But they don't want to officially break up, either. They don't explicitly talk about their plan. Their plan is to just—see what happens.

Elyse has never visited before and asks to see all the places from his past. Rom shows her his elementary school, and the playground structure he would hide under to avoid bullies. He shows her his high school, the square, brick monolith that looks like a factory.

They walk through the park and he points to where the punks used to hang out, or where the homeless would sleep, or where art students would paint landscapes by the slow, curving brook. Many of these hidden nooks have been replaced by playgrounds, sprinklers for kids, or community gardens. The elevated tracks are still being dismantled, leaving shadows over parts of the paths and rivers.

"So, this is how you walked home from school?" Elyse clutches his hand.

"Yup." He nods.

He doesn't say anything about Magnolia or how they'd spend their afternoons together.

"And this whole place fills up in the summer for a festival?"

"Yeah, I used to go when I was a kid. There are rides and local restaurants set up stalls and there are street performers. It's actually pretty fun." He stops himself from adding, *It's too bad you won't be here.*

He doesn't say it, but maybe she senses it, because she squeezes him closer to her.

Rom brings Elyse downtown, where the buildings stand tall and people in suits rush along the sidewalk. Bike messengers cut between the flow of towncars and cabs. Rom stops at the corner and points to a skyscraper made of black glass.

"That's where he wants you to work?"

"Unfortunately."

When Rom finished college, his father gave him a new watch.

"A man's accessory," his father said.

But Rom doesn't wear it, and doesn't feel any less like a man.

Rom and Elyse visit museums and go window-shopping. She admires the quaint architecture, noting how different each part of the city is from each other. Rom notices with disappointment that many of his favorite local shops and restaurants have been replaced by chain stores. They return to the apartment in the basement and cool off with a shower together before cooking dinner in the little kitchen.

He imagines what it might be like if she stayed, but he doesn't broach the subject. They've been having such a good time that he doesn't want to wreck it by talking about things that make them sad. They had one conversation about it, a couple months before graduation. But they reached an impasse, and never bothered to talk about it again.

The night before she has to leave, they go out to dinner with Rom's father. Rom had tried to get them out of it, but his father insisted, and Elyse thought it would be fun.

"Why don't you wear the watch?" she suggests as they get ready in the apartment.

"I dunno," Rom says. "It's not really my style."

She slips it on his wrist.

"It actually looks pretty good on you," she tells him. "That's a really nice gift."

But really, Rom knows that it's a shackle.

They spend dinner with his father and girlfriend chatting more with each other than Rom. Rom sits by, silent but not sulking, as they agree so easily about politics and the state of the world.

Then they turn to him.

Elyse agrees with Rom's father, that he should go to work. That he would be a great asset to the company. That it's time for him to take part in the family business.

Rom nods along, saying, "Maybe."

He assumes this is some sort of ruse she's playing, that when they return to the apartment, Elyse will kick-off her high heels and tell him that his father is stuffy and full of crap.

But she doesn't.

"I think your father is right," she says. "You should start working for him."

"Are you serious?"

"Yeah, I am," she says. "Look at this—you have such a great setup. You live in this great apartment in this beautiful city, and you have a job lined up for you. Most people our age would kill for this kind of opportunity."

Rom is skeptical.

"Why not just try it?" she asks. "You can always quit."

Rom knows once he starts, he will never be able to quit.

"Just, go. In the morning. After I leave."

She says this last part a little softer, reminding him that it is their last night together, and soon it will be over. He takes her hand and pulls her onto the couch, where they make love and fall asleep.

In the morning, he asks, "Are you sure you don't want a ride to the airport?"

"Yeah, it's better this way."

He calls for a taxi and they cuddle while they wait for it to arrive.

Rom watches from the porch as she walks down the brick path to the cab waiting in the driveway.

After placing her suitcase in the trunk and slamming it shut, she turns and calls out, "We're going to see each other again, right?"

"Of course," he says.

Elyse gets into the cab and shuts the door. He looks on as it pulls around the circular landscaping and down the driveway. Then he turns to go back inside. Rom puts his hand on the doorknob, but stops, noticing the gleaming watch on his wrist.

He had forgotten to take it off the night before, and remembers that he told Elyse that he would go to his father's office. Already he is being led down a path that he doesn't want to take. He turns from the house and follows the driveway, unstrapping the watch from his wrist and tucking it into his pocket.

On the street, he keeps walking.

It's mid-morning on a Tuesday and the park is empty. Usually there are people jogging or walking their dogs or parents looking on as their kids run around the playground. Everyone must be at work. Rom could have been among them. Instead, he buys a used paperback at the bookstore for 50 cents, his small contribution to the local economy, which he knows basically adds up to nothing.

He tucks his book into the back of his pants and jumps up to climb a tree. Settled on a comfortable perch, his legs extended on either side of a wide branch like riding a horse, he leans back against the trunk and opens the book.

Rom is still reading when the air begins to smell intensely of sweet blossoms. It doesn't make sense. Spring has passed and the flowers are gone, replaced by grass and leaves that share the same, deep-summer green. But this aroma is so thick it becomes hard to breathe. His nostrils flare to suck in oxygen. He looks up and sees a figure walking along the bike path, moving with a familiar, easy gait. Even from a distance and up in a tall tree, he can recognize Magnolia, her gaze cast low, just beyond her feet like she's looking for something.

"Hey!" he shouts out. "I know you!"

She looks up, startled.

He waves.

She shields her eyes and without the glare of the sun she must register who he is because she calls back, "What are you doing up there?"

"Reading!" He holds up his book.

"Aren't you worried about falling over?"

"Nah." He climbs down to a lower limb and drops to the ground. They approach each other and hug so hard he lifts her off her feet, even though she's just a speck taller than him.

"It's been a long time," she says as he lowers her back down to the ground.

"Yeah." He nods, then notices the familiar bag slung across her chest. "You still have that?"

"You know me," she says. "I don't get rid of stuff that easy."

"What do you have in there?"

"Secrets," she says.

"Good."

There's a pause. They had seen each other's updates online, but it was the type of friendship that didn't interact beyond the occasional 'Like.' Rarely a comment. He doesn't know what to say next.

"Can I hang out? For a while?" she asks.

"Of course." He sinks to the ground. "Be my guest."

She stoops down, folding her legs under herself to sit with him.

Under the shade cast by the tall oak, they pick at the grass, talking about nothing in particular. He notices how the uniform she wore in high school—a button-down blouse and pleated skirt—have been replaced by black leggings and a gray, oversized sweater. She still wears those heavy, black boots. She still has those gauged ears. But her hair is different, no longer dyed bright colors. Her hair's natural color is faded, with the roots growing in dark. It's tousled, still bed-headed. She looks tired.

"So, how's Elyse?"

"Good, I think."

"You think?"

"She came to visit for a while, but she left today."

She turns to look at Rom, but the morning sun is behind him, so she has to squint. "Are you guys fighting or something?"

"No, I mean, I guess we're technically broken up."

"Oh. Sorry."

"It's okay. We're just, seeing what happens, you know?"

She nods, but doesn't say much. Rom recalls the last time he saw Magnolia. She didn't say much then, either. She isn't as guarded, but something about her feels distant, like she's sank deeper into the quiet part of herself, leaving him wondering what happened to the girl who laughed loudly and rambled about interesting nonsense.

She asks, "So, what else is new with you?"

"My dad got rid of all my stuff."

"That sucks."

"Yeah."

"My mom never touched any of my things. Mount Vesuvius couldn't have preserved it better." She yanks a dandelion out of the grass and asks, "What in particular did he get rid of?"

"Pretty much everything. My posters. My furniture. Old school projects. Picture books from when I was really little. My record collection. I'm pretty bummed about that."

"Understandably."

He watches her twirl the dandelion between her fingers, waiting for her to blow the puffy seeds into the wind.

She doesn't.

He continues, "You'd think he would have been like—'Vinyl? Classy. I should really keep that to show how sophisticated I am.' But he didn't."

"Well, were they, like, punk albums?"

"Not at all. It was mostly jazz and classical."

Heat swells as the breeze fades. He wonders if Magnolia is hot in her outfit, but doesn't ask. He says, "What kills me is that he knew I'd be coming back—he even *wanted* me to come back. Why would he get rid of all my stuff?"

"Maybe he thought you wanted it like that? You know, an actual apartment. Not some teenage boy bedroom."

Rom stops and considers that.

"Shit. You're probably right," he says, thinking of his father's gifts and gestures, which always seemed for a version of Rom who didn't exist. "You should be a therapist."

Magnolia lets out a sudden, sarcastic laugh. It rises into hysterics, more like the girl he remembers. He smiles too, laughter breaking through his grin.

They sit and talk until the sun sets and the cicadas' unified cry rings its mechanical shrill. These summer days stretch out longer and longer, sunlight bleeding into the night. They say good-bye in orange twilight. The trees and buildings around them are hazy silhouettes.

Magnolia's throat scratches after hours of talking, and laughing. She reaches in her bag for a cigarette, even though she knows that smoke won't soothe. The lighter isn't as easily accessible, and she steps aside on the sidewalk to make room for passers-by, even though there's no one in the street.

She reaches into the depths of her bag. She hadn't used it since high school and had forgotten how deceptive it is, like there's more room inside than appears. Her fingers touch something metal, and she digs for it, thinking it's her lighter. She pulls out a locket instead.

A brass, heart-shaped locket that she once found on the sink of a public bathroom, a locket that Zane would use to hide pills—two at a time. She doesn't want to know if there's anything inside. She throws the locket into the gutter, and searches faster for the lighter, now desperate for the cigarette that's poised between her teeth.

She lights it, the nicotine rushing fast to her head in a satisfying buzz. She hadn't smoked the entire time she was with Rom. She didn't even notice if she had a craving.

Magnolia walks under the street lights casting their burnt yellow glow. She remembers how, when she was a kid, she was allowed to play outside until the street lights came on. There weren't many rules growing up, but that was one she could not defy. Now, an adult, she knows she should go home.

But she's starting to remember how to be a person again.

And she worries that if she goes home, she'll forget.

Home never changed, which is comforting, but also sickening, cloying—like that last bite of cake that you regret after a big dinner. She knows that she'll return to the sound of baseball on TV. A fan whirring in the corner, but not doing anything to cool the air in the small house. Her feet sticking on the kitchen linoleum. Her mom folding laundry and drinking something cold, the ice cubes softly clacking against each other and the side of her big plastic cup as she takes another sip.

Her mother would worry if she knew that Magnolia was out here, by the station, alone, at night.

She stands on the overpass, leans her arms against the railing, looks down at the street below. A car rushes by, its headlights adding to the flood of light as it passes. She watches her breath float into the dark.

What is she going to tell her mom?

She met up with a friend.

It isn't a lie.

Rom is a friend. A good friend. And she almost forgot about him. Things hadn't been the same after she left school. He never came back to visit during college, either—especially after he started going out with Elyse. And she was preoccupied with Zane.

It occurs to her that Rom has no idea what happened. Rom had hung out with the AV Club kids who played D&D, not Zane's group of colorful burn-outs and brilliant anarchists. The likelihood of it coming up on his newsfeed was slim.

It's been a long time since they'd spoken, but she's sure that he would have said something, if he knew.

Seeing Rom reminded her of what it was like for someone to be happy to see her. He had always offered this reassuring presence when they hung out together—which was a lot, their junior year of high school. She always felt like she could be herself with him.

She takes a drag on her cigarette and remembers one of the first conversations they had.

Rom had told her to quit.

Then she remembers, with a sick feeling, how many times she had asked Zane to quit. How she would worry about him—how she pleaded with him. It never really got him to stop. And even once he stopped, he didn't really change.

She stares down at the cigarette burning between her fingers. She doesn't want to be the kind of person that leaves her loved ones begging. She flicks the cigarette away, watching it fall onto the street below. It bounces off the pavement, sparks flying as the cherry breaks loose. Then it's gone, too small and insignificant for her to see. Her heart goes into a panic thinking that it might be her last cigarette, and it wasn't even finished.

Magnolia instinctively reaches into her bag for her pack. She stares down at the small box with worn corners still wrapped in plastic. She knows that she could pull out a fresh one—but instead she drops the pack to the sidewalk and crushes it with her boot before throwing it into a nearby trash can.

She has the perfect distraction from Zane, from not smoking, from figuring out the rest of her life. She has a plan. She texts Rom.

There's a shortcut that goes through the woods, eventually leading to a set of stairs that end at the distant rear of his dad's property. But Rom takes the long way home, following side streets that curve around the hill leading up to his father's house. As he climbs, the houses get farther apart, and the cars disappear behind driveways, then the driveways are blocked by gates, and the sidewalk turns into a dirt path. The old gas lamps shine white, illuminating the green leaves against the twilight sky. His phone buzzes in his pocket. The caller ID reads:

Elyse

"Hey."

Her voice is like honey at the other end of the line. Thick and sweet and comforting. He smiles to hear her voice and starts pacing circles in the empty street. She tells him about her trip, what her day was like, the things she had seen.

"I miss you," she tells him.

"Me too," he says.

"What have you been up to?"

He tells her about the book he started reading. He doesn't say anything about Magnolia.

"How was the office today? Not as bad as you thought, right?"

"I didn't go."

"Oh, why not?" Her voice is suddenly sharper, losing its lusciousness.

It's hard for him to explain how he knows he didn't get the job because he has skills or savvy. He never earned the job, or his father's respect. He knows his father would be able to control him, and he would always be a child.

"Well, I should probably get going," she interrupts, not bothering to hear his explanation.

"Okay. We'll talk later?"

"Yeah."

They hang up. Rom thinks back to last night, how she was by his side, filling the basement with laughter. The way her fist clutched the neck of a wine bottle as she worked a corkscrew. Undoing the long zipper down the back of her dress. How she had gripped the sofa as she moved on top of him. The curve of her body snug against his while they slept.

His phone chimes and he smiles, thinking of Elyse. But when he looks down, the message is from Magnolia. He's a little surprised, but pleased.

Do you want to go back to the in-between place?

Rom has to re-read the message a couple times before believing that it's real. They had spent the whole day together, talking, but never mentioned the in-between place. But now that she suggests going there, his pulse quickens, a light sweat breaks along his brow. A distant but familiar feeling of nerves and excitement.

He wonders if it's a good idea.

He decides not to question it.

Okay. When do you want to go?

He kicks pebbles across the street as he waits for her response. He doesn't want to assume that she wants to go right away. Maybe she'll want to go home, think about it. Maybe they'll go later in the week. He'll be happy to go whenever she wants. He thought that they would never go back.

Now.

Now he wonders why he had to choose the long way home. He walks back down the hill, the houses getting closer together and the gardens between them narrowing and cars again left parked on the street.

He feels a little guilty, switching gears from talking to Elyse—and missing her, and thinking of their last night together—to meeting up with Magnolia. He reminds himself that he isn't doing anything wrong. He and Magnolia are friends. He told himself, years ago, that they would only ever be friends, and closed the door on the hope that they would ever be more.

Magnolia is already by the station. In high school, when she was alone, she never looked like she was bored or waiting. But she does now, standing by the overpass, looking at the street below. There's something about her that seems sad to him. Something about the way she stands makes it look like she's trying to be smaller.

But when she sees him approach, she smirks, her eyes a little daring. She asks, "You ready?"

The ground below them shakes and rumbles as a train goes by.

They approach the gate. There are some low shrubs and broken concrete. The ground in front of it is overrun with leaves that no one had raked away after winter. It was always open to them, but this time it's barred shut.

"Here, why don't we do this," he says, and reaches up to grip the bars.

He hikes himself up, pressing his sneakers against the gate, then climbs up and over the top. His feet thud onto the dirt path. He turns, expecting to see her climbing too, but Magnolia is still standing on the other side. Her fists clench like she's tempted, but she's hesitating.

She bites her lip and grips the bars, imitating Rom's movements, but it takes her a couple more kicks up the iron to get over the top.

The path is dark and hard to walk. It's quiet between trains. Just the sound of their steps in the black night. She trips and catches herself on his shoulder, and he reaches out to help her gain her balance, his hand brushing against her waist.

"I'm fine," she says before he can ask if she's okay.

They reach the wall of ivy, running their hands under, searching for the door. Magnolia flashes her phone to find the doorknob.

"You open it," she tells him.

Rom presses down on the latch and pushes the door. White light escapes through the crack as it opens, so bright against the darkness that they have to shield their eyes as they enter.

THE DISMISSAL BELL PIERCED through the building, vibrating her bones. Magnolia stepped into the crowded hallway, clutching the strap of her bag, the desire to be near Zane clawing inside her ribs. She wanted his arm hooked around her waist, the warmth off his body pressed against hers, the faint smell of his deodorant. It felt like forever since they had been alone, together.

He used to hold her hand and sneak them into the movies. He liked horror movies, and even though they gave her nightmares, she never complained. She used it as an excuse to curl closer into him, admiring the way the light and shadows flickered across his face. He brought her to rooftops to look out at the city lights, moving and sparking below.

He told her things like, *I was a mess before I met you.*

Or, *If you weren't here, I would be broken.*

Then he would hug her close, and everything felt like it would be okay.

He used to follow along as she looked for lost objects. She liked it best when he made up stories for how things went missing, and who used to possess them, and what those people were doing now without their things. But Zane had started getting restless, urging her back to the park so he could be with his friends.

He was someone else when they were with his friends, someone who didn't notice her.

She would sit, silent, by his side.

Zane used to walk her home, but since the start of this school year, she'd had to wait longer for him to stand up and say bye to his friends. This past week she'd had to go home without him, and she was getting used to this brand of loneliness—a feeling more akin to nausea. She tried to cling closer to him. The further he pulled back, the more urgently she wanted to fill the space between them.

The afternoon was sticky as summer, even though it was September, and Magnolia's uniform blazer was stifling. But being with Zane was more urgent, and she scanned the crowd for him. It was easy to spot his friends, whose colorful mohawks and half-shaved heads and altered uniforms covered in punk patches and safety pins stood out among their classmates milling in gray uniforms.

Zane didn't alter his uniform, and looked handsome in it, with his sleeves rolled up, the blazer tossed over his shoulder.

He didn't smile when their eyes met across the crowd. She knew that he was going to tell her something bad. She went to him and slipped her hand into his. He held it, but it wasn't a loving squeeze. More like holding a drink for someone while they went to the bathroom.

They followed behind as the group trekked to their favorite spot at the park, by the curve in the brook with the wall of reeds that shielded their activities from anyone passing on the road behind them. He didn't drop her hand, which she took as a good sign. But he stopped before the clearing.

"Maggie," he said, and sighed. She knew what was coming, but didn't want to say it for him. "I think I need some time alone."

"You're breaking up with me?"

"Well, not breaking up exactly," he told her. "But I need a break."

She could see his friends over his shoulder—sitting and smoking—ready for another afternoon that she had always considered boring. Now she wanted nothing more than to join them. Except Zane was standing like a roadblock.

"What do you mean 'a break'?"

"I just need some time. I should just hang out with the guys and do my thing—alone," he told her. "We're all going to go to college soon, and then it's not going to be the same anymore."

She wanted to tell him, *It's not going to be the same with us, either*. That he would be leaving her, too. That she wasn't sure what was going to happen to them, after he graduated.

But she didn't say anything.

He offered her a limp hug, nothing like the way it used to be, but she held on anyway. She watched as he walked away. What was she supposed to do now? She didn't want to go home. Anyone who she had considered a friend was behind her, with him. Which got her asking herself, *What is school going to be like tomorrow?*

Magnolia reached into her bag and pulled out a pack of cigarettes. She had found them and held onto them, thinking she could give them to Zane's friends.

But that didn't matter anymore.

She pulled one out of the pack and put it between her lips. Then lit it with an antique lighter. She coughed out smoke, then took another drag.

Rom was taking his time going home from school that day.

He'd met with his guidance counselor, who'd told him that he wasn't an "ideal applicant" with his current transcripts. She had suggested he try some more extracurriculars, to show some more range in his interests, and that he pull his grades up.

He didn't want to tell his father about the meeting. Even though his dad wouldn't be home when Rom arrived, he didn't want to sit in his room and wait for the conversation, the long lecture, and later, the constant reminders of how he needed to apply himself.

It was also a warm afternoon and nice to feel the fresh air after being in the dusty school building. He walked along the shady paths in the park. Then he saw Magnolia. She walked with determination, or maybe it just seemed like that because of her heavy black boots. Her stockings were ripped and the skirt of her uniform was hiked higher than the other girls at school. She was taller than he realized. Practically his height, he noted as he walked by. Maybe even taller. He turned his head to double check, just as she exhaled a puff of smoke.

"You shouldn't smoke," he said, coughing. Then he clenched his mouth shut. He hadn't said anything to this girl in the entire year they had been in the same class—why did he have to say *that?* She was never going to talk to him. He lowered his gaze and watched his sneakers move across the footpath, faster than before.

"I don't."

He turned back and saw her standing, the gray jacket of her uniform draped over one arm, the other cocked and posed as a cigarette burned between her fingers. She took a drag.

He had told himself he wasn't going to say anything more, and would do his best to disappear, but suddenly felt like he had nothing to lose. "What do you mean, you don't—you're smoking right now."

She looked down at the cigarette still fuming between her fingers. "I mean, I'm smoking, but I'm not a smoker."

"What's the difference?"

"I've never bought my own pack." She coughed, or maybe dramatically cleared her throat, he couldn't tell.

He told her, "But you're still doing it."

She stared at him. The same unwavering gaze she cast when she first arrived at school. "Aren't you in my homeroom?" she asked.

"Yeah."

"What's your name again?"

"Rom."

"What kind of name is that?"

He shrugged. He noticed a flicker in her expression when he didn't fight back. He could tell that she was sorry, even though she didn't say anything. "Why don't you go by Magnolia?"

"What? How do you know my real name?"

"I just, remembered. From last year—" he stammered and blushed. "On the first day, teachers called you that when they took roll call. Then after a day or two they switched to

Maggie." She kept staring. He kept talking, "I didn't know it was you at first. It was weird. I was like, who's Maggie? Did we get another transfer student or something? Then I realized it was you."

He added, "I didn't really get it. I thought Magnolia was way cooler."

"Really?"

"Yeah, I mean, there are plenty of Maggies, but you don't really hear about too many Magnolias."

"Well, thanks. I guess I was always made fun of for it. So, I tried to stop it. You know?"

"Yeah, kids suck. But, you can't let that stop you from being you."

The dismissal bell rang and she walked out of the building in slow motion. Everyone else had someone to talk to—or a cluster of friends—moving together, with a sense of purpose, belonging. But for her, it was like her first day of school all over again.

She hadn't been planning on becoming Zane's girlfriend. She didn't want to be anyone's girlfriend—or even anyone's friend.

The afternoon before her first day at school, she'd gone to the beauty supply store. She dyed her hair red and purple, leaving streaks of platinum untouched. In the morning, she lined her eyes with thick pencil and pulled on a pair of ripped fishnets that she bought and destroyed.

No one had dared approach the transfer student, the new punk girl. They were too intimidated. She liked it better that way.

But at lunch, Zane had flagged her down to sit with him and his friends, and it was her turn to be intimidated.

She may have looked like a punk, but she didn't know anything about being a punk. She didn't know the bands that they were talking about. She didn't have their same attitude or sense of humor. She maintained her guise by not saying anything.

Being silent had only added to her mysteriousness. After school, they'd waved her down again, asking her to come with them to the park. Zane kept her close to his side, which was strange—but exciting.

Magnolia hadn't noticed how much she had been using Zane as a social shield—a crutch, really—until he was gone.

She ate lunch alone in the library, careful to not leave any crumbs on the carpet by the old reference books. She felt raw but didn't cry, and did her best to not look at Zane as they passed each other in the halls. She pretended that he didn't exist, that they never knew one another. He was just another stranger—except less. Strangers intrigued her. She wanted Zane to mean nothing.

After school, with the rest of the day long and empty in front of her, she ached for his company. But more, she wanted to be somebody. Alone, she felt like no one.

She lit a cigarette—a new tic she discovered to smolder the burning inside—and walked toward the park. *Not to see Zane*, she reminded herself. She would go about what she always did—or wanted to do, but couldn't because she was waiting for him. She would take a walk and think and find new places and lost objects.

And, maybe he would see her and feel like an idiot for dumping her.

Sun glittered in the leaves, but there were spots where the foliage was starting to turn gold and red. Some trees had already turned completely yellow. She walked the footpath that led to her neighborhood, but told herself that if she found any turn or place to stray from the path, to take it.

Except she'd already explored all the paths in the park, and there was nothing new or unknown.

Rom was walking, too. His hands were in his pockets and his shoulders were slightly slouched. His friends all wore polished shoes with their uniforms, but he wore navy high tops with loose laces. She had kept thinking about him, his comments, the way he didn't seem afraid to tell her what he thought, but still had a meek personality.

It was strange, but in a good way.

She tossed her cigarette and ran to catch up with him.

"How come you don't take the train like everyone else?" she asked.

He looked up at her, startled, his eyes wide behind his glasses.

He didn't say anything, so she continued, "The train's a lot faster than walking."

"It's more peaceful to walk," he said.

They looked back at a group of their classmates, who were laughing and pushing at each other. They didn't want to squeeze into the train with them. They didn't want to listen to the kids shouting and holding up the train as they jumped on and off between cars.

"I understand."

"How come you don't take the train?"

"I guess there's no reason to rush home, you know?"

He nodded. "Yeah."

He couldn't believe that she had approached him, that she was talking to him and walking next him. He felt himself stare, making sure that she was real and this was really happening. He eventually found the words to answer her questions and continue the conversation. Then she fell silent, and he didn't know what to say.

She stooped down and picked up a wire hanger, and continued to walk, tilting her face toward the sky to bask in the afternoon sun.

"What are you doing with that?" he asked, glad to finally have a topic of conversation.

"With what?" Her eyes were still closed, her expression serene.

"That hanger you just picked up."

"Oh—I dunno." She shrugged. "It didn't belong on the ground though." And then she changed the subject, saying, "Did you know a cloud weighs as much as an elephant?"

"I didn't," he said. "Is that true?"

"I think so," she said. "But I can't remember where I learned it."

"How does that even work?" he asked. "An elephant wouldn't be able to float in the sky."

"No, but water isn't an elephant."

"Or water vapor, you mean?"

"I guess."

She stopped again, this time focusing on a row of bushes along the iron fence that dropped down to the subway tracks below. He watched as she crossed the grass, her bag rocking against the sway of her hips.

"What is it?" he asked, still standing on the path as she crouched low and reached under one of the shrubs, pulling out a yellow tie.

"I don't know how to tie a tie," she told him.

Rom took the tie, which had a cruddy feel to the fabric, and made the loop—a skill he learned from years of wearing a uniform. He felt her studying his fingers, but he wasn't sure if she was trying to learn how to tie, or if she was capturing something else entirely.

"Good!" she said when he handed it back to her. "Now all we need is a shirt. And some pants."

They continued to walk and ponder out loud about elephants and clouds. Rom kept his gaze to the ground, even though he doubted that they would find any more clothes. He noticed how Magnolia wasn't even looking, she was too busy telling him about how elephants had funerals.

And then she found a shirt.

She put the shirt on the hanger, and wrapped the tie under the collar like a display at a department store. They left the outfit hanging on a chain-link fence.

"Someone will use it," she said.

The train rumbled below, and they passed under the long-unused elevator tracks. The trolley used to make a loop around the city, but it had been replaced by a more efficient subway system. The elevated tracks still hadn't been dismantled. The arches and supports were rusted, and dried puddles left stains on the pavement. It was dark, but light cracked through the old tracks above them.

"The city should really take this down," he said.

"Why?"

"It's pointless now," he said. "And it was always pretty ugly."

The shadows of the former tracks eventually gave way to sunshine.

"I'm going to miss it," she said. Her voice was softer, lacking the forceful enthusiasm it showed when she was talking about elephants.

"Really? Why?"

"I liked how it was—I don't like it when things change."

"How come?" he asked.

"Because when things change, they become easier to forget about. It makes me feel like that could happen to me," she told him. "I don't ever want to be forgotten."

They did it again the next day. Same roaming walk, same aimless banter. Except this time her hair was bright blue with a streak of yellow.

Their walks became an automatic part of their routine. When they were both starting to get tired during their afternoon classes, they would wonder—what would they talk about together? What would they see during their walks? What new things would they come across?

They would meet outside the building and start walking. One of them would start a conversation with some sort of non-sequitur that they had been mulling over during the last class period.

"Sometimes I wish I didn't know how to talk."

"Do you ever wonder what your life would be like if you dropped out?"

"Life would be pretty different if we had gills instead of noses."

Sometimes they would break into uncontrollable laughter. Sometimes their debates got heated. Sometimes, they didn't say anything at all.

He marveled at how she found things—postcards and old photos. Books. A record. Keychains. A fanny pack. A teddy bear with the tag still on it. When she picked up a twenty dollar bill, they went to a diner and ate pancakes. It was a little awkward, to sit and not move. They didn't make eye contact. Their conversation was more clipped and choppy than their usual coasting banter.

It felt like a first date.

They walked together until they reached a block of row houses—narrow, tall, and brick—that separated their neighborhood. Inside, everyone knew, the houses were a sort of patchwork of rich and poor. Some were remodeled with the original woodwork restored and new, state of the art amenities. Other buildings

were split into apartments that smelled wet
and musty and had all sort of problems.

But everyone knew the places with problems would eventually go away.

The row houses were the last landmark before the station, their signal to start wrapping
up their conversation and not end their walk
on an awkward note.

They never invited each other over to their
houses. They were too embarrassed to show
where they came from, but also didn't want
their nice walks to turn into something more
complicated.

Life already felt complicated enough.

"Hey—" She looked at something over his
shoulder. "Have you ever noticed that gate
before?"

Rom turned to look. Past the station was
an iron gate, slightly open. The type of thing
he wouldn't have noticed if he was walking on
his own.

"You wanna check it out?" he asked, even
though he already knew her answer.

Commuters leaving the train station dispersed, leaving Rom and Magnolia to walk unnoticed through the gate. Past the gate was a
narrow dirt path crowded by overgrowth of
urban plants—weeds and bramble branches

and messy grass. Trees loomed above them, the bare branches brown and gray, except for the fluffy evergreens that were too thick to see through.

The path travelled parallel to the tracks. They could hear the train rumble and screech on the rails below. Rom and Magnolia kept walking. It wasn't long before they reached a tall stone wall, its surface rough and covered with moss and ivy.

"Well, I guess we have to go back," he said.

Magnolia didn't turn to leave. She reached out to sweep aside a tall curtain of ivy, revealing a door. She turned back to him, grinning.

"Go on," he said. "Open it."

She opened the door and made her way through. Rom followed, the vines knocking against his glasses.

Beyond the door was nothing special. The path continued, the same vegetation growing as on the other side of the wall. The temperature though, was significantly colder, sweeping through their fall jackets. Their breath came out in puffs of white.

"Wow—why is it so cold?" he asked, shivering.

"I dunno—let's run to keep warm!"

She darted off, not waiting for his answer. He had no choice but to follow as she raced deeper into the woods. He ran fast, looking out for rocks or roots that could trip him. When he looked up, he saw that she had stopped moving. Her body still, the blue and yellow of her hair a strange contrast to the distant evergreens. He stood by her, catching his breath, and looked to see what had captivated her attention.

A small tree with pink blossoms adorning its delicate branches stood in the middle of the woods. Snow fell from the gap in the canopy above them, resting on the branches but not accumulating.

"This is weird," he said.

"It's amazing."

They stood and watched until the heat in their bodies faded and they began shivering again. Then she picked up one of the flowers that had fallen off the branch and carefully tucked it into her bag. They turned around to go home.

The phone was ringing when he got home, echoing in the marble foyer. It was never for him, so he didn't bother picking up. He went down to the basement, still chilled from their walk in the woods, and wrapped himself in his blanket. The phone wasn't stopping, so he threw off the blanket and answered, "Yeah?"

"Rom?"

It was her.

"Hey—Magnolia?"

"Yeah, it's me. Look, I got locked out of my house. I think I dropped my keys."

"Oh, really?"

"Yeah—" There was a pause. "You know. At that place."

"Oh." He understood. "Well, we should go back, then?"

"Yeah."

"Do you want to meet me at that door?"

"Um—okay."

"Or—I can come find you?"

"Yeah, I'm at the train station."

"Okay, I'll be right down."

She wasn't at the train station. She'd called from the payphone at the corner store next to her house.

Everyone who lived on this side of the city knew there was the part where the wealthy people lived. Refurbished Victorian houses were painted elegant or funky colors, with lush, manicured gardens and old gas lamps lit the street. And there was the part of town for everyone else.

Magnolia and her mom had their own house, but she didn't want Rom to see the rest of her neighborhood—the trash in the hedges or the stains on the sidewalks or the signs in shop windows saying that they accept food stamps. She didn't want him to see how she lived by the police station, how the cruisers were constantly patrolling, flashing their lights, pulling people over.

That crime here was real, that this was where the bad things actually happened—that it was a reality, not just something discussed over catered dinners on real china and tapered candles.

She could tell from the way he looked at her that he respected her. She didn't want him to not look at her that way anymore. She didn't want a place to change the way he saw her.

He could see her standing on the overpass, her blue hair waving in the breeze. He didn't understand why she called him. She seemed so fearless. She didn't need him. His heart had started racing when he'd heard her voice on the other end of the line and it was still strumming fast in his chest, tingles like electricity going up his shoulders and down his spine.

"This is so stupid," she seethed.

"What is?" he asked, maybe a little too fast.

She didn't seem to notice the earnest tone in his voice. Or if she did, she ignored it.

"I *never* lose anything."

"It's pretty inconvenient," he said. "I lose things all the time."

"I *never* lose my stuff."

"I'm sure we'll find them," he tried to reassure her.

They kept their eyes on the ground, scanning the sidewalk for a pile of glinting metal.

Nothing.

He imagined a different Magnolia, picking up her keys and treasuring them forever in a jar with other lost keys.

"So, I guess they're in the place," he said. "Unless they're at school."

"I'm not going back to school now."

They stood in front of the wall of ivy, brushing past its hanging vines, but they couldn't find the door beyond it.

"What the hell," she said, running her hands along the surface.

"What?" he asked, stepping back to see if he could see over the top. "What's wrong?"

She pulled the vines aside where the door had been, but it was flat with the facade of wood and metal adornments painted on the wall.

"That was a door earlier. And we went in there." She started to back away. "I think we should get out of here."

"But what about your keys?"

"Fuck my keys," she said. "This is creeping me out."

His mouth went dry and he swallowed. "Okay—I can walk you back?"

"No, I'm good."

She turned to walk and he was mortified. What had he done wrong? It wasn't his fault they found a door and now it wasn't a door. He looked over his shoulder. Her shock of hair was walking farther along the path.

"Dammit," he cursed, kicking the wall.

Through the ivy, he heard hinges creak open. When he pulled the ivy aside, the door was back, open again, cold exhaling into the air. A rush of excitement and anticipation warmed his stomach.

"Magnolia!" he yelled. "Magnolia!"

He didn't want to leave the doorway, he didn't know if it would change again. He knew that was crazy to think, but he needed her to witness it, to know for himself that it was real.

"What?" she yelled back. He waved her down.

She returned, stunned. They went back inside.

"Holy shit."

The woods were gone.

A cold wind kicked dust into their faces, stirring debris across the narrow street covered with broken glass and shattered pieces of buildings. The street lamps were knocked over sideways. There was a buzz like static and the air reeked of sulfur.

"What is this?"

"I dunno, but I think your keys are gone."

They stood together. She clutched his arm with both her hands.

Rom wondered if she did it because she was scared. Or maybe she got dizzy. Either way, he held himself tall and sturdy. He imagined himself becoming the kind of man that someone could depend on.

"Let's go." Her voice sounded strange. He'd never heard her so serious, or scared.

"Okay." He backed up to turn around and go home.

"No—" She held his arm tighter. "Let's go in."

Rubble crunched under their feet as they walked past buildings with brick bleached pink or charred black. Doors hung off their hinges, revealing dark shadows inside. She turned to look into the buildings as they passed, not letting go of his arm.

The sun was setting, staining the sky and glowing orange and yellow in the remaining windows. It was like the city had been pulled inside out, with beds and dressers dumped onto the sidewalk, crushing the trees that once lined the street. Grass and weeds grew through the broken pavement. She released her grip on his arm to jump over a wide crack in the street, but grabbed his hand when he made it to her side. Both their palms were clammy.

He wasn't sure what he was more preoccupied with—this ruined neighborhood around them, or the feel of her hand in his. He thought that she would let go—but she didn't. Neither did he.

"Look," she said, pointing at a row of buildings, identical to the row houses they always passed near the station. The windows on the lowest level had the same iron roses adorning the black bars, and the remaining cement steps were painted the same ruddy brown.

"You don't think—" He wanted to ask if she thought they were the same buildings, but he knew it was impossible. They had just passed them, not even an hour before, and they were still intact.

"Maybe we should go inside," she suggested.

"I don't think that's a good idea," Rom told her. "We don't want a roof to collapse on us, or anything."

She didn't say anything. She let go of his hand and said, "We should go home."

He agreed, and they retraced their steps back to the door.

The sun had set, leaving the path dark and difficult to navigate. The air felt colder, too. Like winter had already arrived. They didn't talk about what they saw. They walked to the station and said good-bye with their usual "See you tomorrow."

The porch light shined in the darkness and all the windows were lit. Magnolia knew her mom was home, and worried. The cold air cut through her tights, but she was already numb.

What did we just see?

Where were we?

She knocked on the front door.

Her mom opened it. "Where have you been?" Her voice was strained. She was still in her white uniform, still wearing her pristine shoes.

"I lost my keys," Magnolia said. "I went looking for them with a friend."

"Zane?"

"Someone else."

Her mom grabbed her close and hugged her.

"Just call next time, okay?"

Magnolia's arms were left limp in her mother's embrace. She worried that her mom would smell the stink of sulfur coming of her skin. Magnolia could still smell it, but her mom didn't seem to notice. Over her mother's shoulder, she could see the clock on the wall.

Its hands pointed to 12:47.

It had only been 4:30 when they'd gone back to the gate—and it didn't seem like they had been there so long.

"I didn't realize it was so late," she said, pulling away from her mother. "I'm sorry."

Magnolia would usually end the conversation and go upstairs, but she felt guilty for upsetting her mother. She stood by the door as her mother returned to the couch, in the blue glow cast by the television.

"How was your day?" Magnolia asked.

"Hard," her mother said. "A kid overdosed tonight. Young guy. Barely looked old enough to drink." Her mom shook her head. "I hope you're being more careful than that."

"Of course," Magnolia told her. She said good night and returned to her room. She collapsed on her bed with her clothes still on.

Then she remembered the flower in her bag. She reached in and pulled it out, the petals still intact and icy in her palm. She put it on the shelf with her other found objects.

She went to sleep, the smell of sulfur soaking into her pillow.

That night Rom drifted somewhere between sleep and wake.

When he closed his eyes, he saw littered streets and collapsed buildings. He had that unsettled feeling like his spine was lifting away from his rib cage.

At school, he knew that he was tired. The words on the silky pages of his textbook made less sense than usual. He knew that his teachers' voices were making noise, but he couldn't make out the words. Static still buzzed in his ears.

He needed to talk to Magnolia.

He kept glancing up at her, trying to will her to acknowledge him, somehow. But she never turned around. They never made eye contact. Even before they found the door and that strange place, she wouldn't look at him. But today he felt especially insignificant.

He started to wonder if he'd just imagined it, which caused his head to spin even more. Did he make it up, or was it part of a fever dream, like what happens when you take an unplanned afternoon nap?

He knew it wasn't.

It had been an afternoon like all their other afternoons. They'd met up outside school, along their route home, and then found the door to that place.

He started to question everything. Were all their walks up until that point part of his imagination?

Had he been delusional in thinking that they had been friends?

Did he just make it all up?

※

In the computer lab, Rom opened a browser to start a web search. He needed to know what the hell it was that they'd seen the day before. Was it just a neighborhood that he never had a reason to check out? Even if it was, it didn't explain why it was in ruins. It didn't seem like it was something that had happened long ago. There were spots that were still smoldering, even some flames slowly burning. And that smell.

The cursor blinked, half-taunting him, but he didn't even know what to search for.

Disaster?

Neighborhood wiped out?

Geological event?

He closed the browser.

He took his time leaving school when the dismissal bell rang, still not sure of where he stood with Magnolia. He started walking down the footpath in the park.

Magnolia caught up to him, breathless, cheeks flushed. "I haven't been able to stop thinking about yesterday."

"I know, me too," he parroted her urgency, glad that they were actually friends and talked to each other.

"And I think we should go back."

"Really? Why?"

"What if there were survivors? Or people who were hurt? Or needed water or something?"

"Magnolia, it didn't seem like anyone was there."

"We should go back," she insisted. "It's the right thing to do."

He knew he couldn't talk her out of it. But he didn't want her to think less of him, and he didn't want Magnolia to get hurt if she went there alone. He followed, but also broke into a sweat.

They walked to the station and passed through the gate. For the third time, they walked along that narrow path and listened to the train rumble along the tracks below. They reached the wall and Magnolia swept the ivy aside to reveal the door.

Again, it was a door.

Why had it ever not been a door? And how did it change back? Was this even happening? Rom stood by with questions as Magnolia swung the door open.

Again, that cold blast of air. And again, a different landscape on the other side.

No dense forests. No destroyed streets.

It was the summer festival. Except the rides sat, rusted and still, their structures like skeletons. There were no people to sit or scream on the rollercoasters. The ferris wheel didn't turn, the merry-go-round didn't spin. They were rusted like they hadn't moved in years. The sky was deep blue with round white clouds that almost looked fake. They were too flat, like they had been painted onto the sky.

Rom burst out laughing.

"What's so funny?" Magnolia asked, acting annoyed by his attitude, but barely able to suppress her smirk.

Rom's laugh bubbled in ripples, forcing his eyes shut. Tears squeezed their way between his eyelashes, and he took his glasses off as he howled.

"Oh god." He held his sides. "Oh god—it hurts."

"I don't see why you're laughing," she said. "This is a serious situation."

"Is serious the word for it?" He cleaned his glasses on his shirt, then adjusted them back on his face. "Crazy is more like it."

"Crazy, serious, whatever," she said. "But there's something wrong here."

"You're right," he said, and made an extra stern face.

She rolled her eyes, but also smiled, and led the way through the stands where there used to be contests and games. The prizes lined on display were broken. The bulbs to the lights were brown and blown out. Carts that sold hot dogs and pretzels and cotton candy were empty, their umbrellas still open, the fabric tattered and stained.

"I don't get it." She turned to Rom, looking helpless. "Every time we come through that door, it has been different. And strange and fucked up."

"Maybe—maybe we just, shouldn't come back here, anymore."

The moment he suggested it, he knew that was the last thing he wanted. Even though the place was strange, it was alluring. Magnolia must have felt that way too, because she looked back at him, hurt.

"We can though," he said. "I just—I don't know. You're right. This place is fucked up."

"It's weird—doesn't this place remind you of the other places?"

"What do you mean?" he asked. "Like that street? And that tree?"

She closed her eyes and he thought that maybe he'd made her mad, but soon she opened her eyes and was smiling at him. She asked, "Do you hear that?"

"What?"

"Every time we come here, there's this white noise," she said. "Listen."

He closed his eyes.

After they left, he walked home, taking the shortcut through the woods to his father's house. The trees were bare and brown leaves covered the ground. The walk up the hill kept him warm, but the skin on his face was cold, despite being flushed—almost sweaty. It had been warm on the other side of the door, although not as hot as it would have been during the actual summer festival.

He kicked his feet through the fallen leaves, enjoying the rustling sound they made as they shifted against the hollow space between them. Then his foot touched something solid, but soft. He reached down and through the blanket of leaves pulled out an old pink teddy bear. It was dirty, and one of its eyes was hanging by a few silky threads.

He smiled, because he'd finally found something he could share with Magnolia. Then he wondered if it had found him.

THE SMOLDERING SUMMER NIGHT breaks into a sharp chill as they step through the door. A chill they remember, a feeling of excitement they both forgot they craved. The door shuts behind them and the cold fades. Their eyes adjust from midnight to daylight.

They stand by the ruins of what looks like a college campus. Vines cover the facades of halls and libraries. The twisting, sprawling ivy has overcome the brick and concrete. Exterior walls are partially knocked down, exposing empty classrooms. Loose debris and cinderblocks are scattered across the footpaths. Weeds and shrubs push through cracks in the pavement. The near-silent static buzzes the way they both remember.

"What do you think?" he asks.

"I'm not sure yet," she says.

They continue to walk. Rom remembers how this has always been the way they conducted their friendship—moving. He thinks about the time they found some money and went out for pancakes. She kept averting her gaze, studying the formica tabletop or staring out the diner window.

They take the crumbling steps into a building. The door lacks weight and claps shut behind them, echoing down the corridor. They peek into classrooms where the vines are climbing through the windows and broken glass has scattered across the floor, where the chairs and desks are still lined up, facing the blackboard, ready for students.

He thinks of Elyse. They ended up alone in a classroom at the end of the previous school year. She had told him that she didn't think they should be together, that they should end things before they got any more serious. He hadn't expected her to break up with him, and was sad for a week before she came back. She had told Rom that she couldn't help herself when it came to him.

"The first time we talked about breaking up, we ended up sitting at a classroom like this," he tells Magnolia.

"Just like this?" She raises an eyebrow and gestures to the dilapidated room around them.

"No—I mean, it was normal," he says. "I just wonder if maybe we should have just ended it then."

"How come?"

"Just seemed like we were probably going to break up anyway," he says. "It would have been one less year to be heartbroken about."

Magnolia nods, and he feels like she can see through him, like he is glass.

They continue through the hallway. The linoleum tiles are covered in dirt and warped from water damage. There aren't any doors on the exit leading out to a quad. Paths point in different directions. They step through the tall grass and lie in the middle.

"So what happened with Zane?" he asks, looking to commiserate.

"It's just—" She swallows hard and looks away. "It didn't work out."

They sit in silence for a while, the sky shifts above them like a kaleidoscope, the blue and gray patches swapping for colors that look more damaged, sallow green and yellow.

Her voice shakes when she speaks again. "Have you ever noticed how there's nothing alive here?"

"We're alive," he says. "And plants are alive."

"Sometimes, but a lot of the time the plants are dead, too."

Rom thinks about it. "We must have seen, like, a fish, once."

"Nope."

"A bird?"

"Nope."

"A three-eyed squirrel?"

"Not even one."

"Hmm." He shrugs. "Why does it matter?"

"It doesn't," she tells him. "It just makes this place even more quiet."

Then neither of them says anything. They both listen to the distant buzz.

"Can you tell me what you remember?"

"From when?"

"From when we used to come here."

He leans back with his hands behind him and looks up at the sky. "You'd think that I'd remember more, but my memory is pretty rotten."

"What do you remember?"

"I remember things in patches. They're like gaseous clouds of emotions that I walk into and sometimes they remind me of something. Otherwise, all I remember really is now."

"Come on," she says. "There has to be something that you remember. Think about it."

"Okay." He closes his eyes. "There was one day we came here, and it was nighttime. Or maybe duskish. Anyway, the moon was rising, and it was blood red."

"Really?" she asks. "Why don't I remember that?"

"Because you fell asleep."

He doesn't say any more and hopes that she won't keep asking about it. Because that was the night that he realized that he loved her, and he had to admit that nothing would ever happen between them. He had looked up at the moon and turned to point it out to her, but saw that she was sleeping. He didn't have the heart to wake her up. And that's when he knew what it meant to love someone. That you cared about them, even if they didn't love you back.

"Well, aren't you special," Magnolia teases him.

Rom smiles, relieved to not have to confess the second part of his story.

"Not special," he says. "Lucky."

When the heat and sun finally make them tired, they brush themselves off and return to the door. It's pre-dawn blue on the other side, with a stillness hovering between night and day. Jumping the gate is harder with the sleep-iness in their hands. She manages with a boost from Rom, then he hops over behind her.

"You gonna be okay going home?" he asks, yawning.

"Yeah."

"We'll hang out later?"

She brightens at his suggestion. "Definitely."

They walk in opposite directions. He turns to make sure she's okay, her figure becoming smaller as she crosses the overpass. She doesn't look back.

She never looked back. That was the nice thing about Elyse, who always came to him, even when he would have preferred to have some space to himself.

Again, he chooses the long way to his father's house, wondering what Elyse is doing right now, if she's just as tired as him. She probably hasn't slept either, still jet-lagged. He has no idea what time it is where she is. He pulls the watch out of his pocket.

The hands move in fast circles, the hour hand revolving in the wrong direction. Rom stares at the face of the watch, trying to make sense of what he's looking at, the ringing getting louder in his ears.

He stops walking and shuts his eyes, a trick he learned from high school.

Sometimes his vision would fool him, especially as they spent more time in the in-between place. If he closed his eyes for long enough, and remembered how things were supposed to be, they'd go back to normal.

He opens his eyes. The watch reads 4:37. He continues to walk, pleased with the grass stains on his sneakers. Now it really feels like summer.

Light from the new day cracks pink through the balcony door, falling faint through the sky-light, onto a new bed. It's as wide as the futon was, low without being on the floor, and covered in pale blue linens she has never seen before.

Her mother must have bought it while Magnolia was out.

Magnolia is so stunned with gratitude that she doesn't want to touch it, doesn't want to make it dirty with her clothes and skin and hair that have been exposed to sun and sweat. The rosy light makes the blue of the sheets almost look violet in the shadows. She rests her hand against the comforter, the fabric cool to the touch.

She has the sudden urge to give her mother a hug. She can't remember the last time she felt compelled to hug her mother, and feels sorry that she hadn't gone with her to get the bed. But maybe her mom would be glad to know that she had talked to someone, that she laughed again.

She looks around her room. There's nothing that doesn't matter to her, that she would dispose of. Taking the old bed away had been a big ordeal. She didn't want to take her room apart, and it was difficult to maneuver down the narrow stairs. She did it anyway, because Zane insisted.

After college, they got a studio downtown. They couldn't afford to come back to their neighborhood, but they wouldn't have returned here, even if they could.

Their studio had three locks on the door, but they only used one. At least, when he was with her. When he went to rehab, she made sure all three were locked and double-checked before going to bed. All they had was the bed and some things for the kitchen that she bought secondhand.

It felt romantic.

Magnolia had told herself that they didn't need much—except each other.

That together, they had everything they could ever need.

She knows now that's not true.

She lies down, reminding herself to thank to her mother in the morning. Her skin tingles with the residue of outside—the smell of grass and sweat.

She falls asleep, telling herself that she doesn't need to worry anymore.

She doesn't notice that the cold pink flower on her shelf is gone.

They meet early in the day. The summer sun is already scalding the sidewalk. Commuters are filing into the station. Men in slacks and button-downs, their bags draped across their chests. Women in sandals and flowing summer skirts, all their possessions for the day squeezed into tote bags. Rom and Magnolia take a moment to acknowledge these people making their way to work. They smile at each other like they have a secret, then hop over the gate and return to the in-between place.

They have a picnic in an abandoned parking lot. The pavement is cracked open with wild-flowers shooting tall around them.

"What about you?" he asks.

"What *about* me?"

"What do you remember?"

"I guess it's like what you said yesterday," she says. "It's more of a feeling than any particular moment."

"What feeling?"

"Powerful." She doesn't even need to think about it, the memory is still strong in her chest. "I felt like we were unstoppable."

He nods.

"What? Is that weird?"

"Not at all," he says. "I actually know exactly what you mean."

"It's just—the rules didn't apply to us. We came here and we could do whatever we wanted. It was freeing."

The in-between place was always waiting for them, but they never knew what to expect on the other side. When they opened the door after school, they could be anywhere—old country towns or abandoned cities, always in a state of decay.

Eventually they realized they didn't have to wait until Monday anymore, they could meet up and hang out at the in-between place all weekend, visiting similar places to where their classmates were hanging out—the mall, old movie theatres, playgrounds at night. Except the places Rom and Magnolia visited were lost in time and overtaken by nature, flowers popping up and green growing over anything that had once been man-made.

After, they would call each other and talk about what they'd seen, sometimes drifting to sleep with their phones pressed to their ears.

Rom knew his father didn't approve of him being out so much, but Magnolia had been helping him with his homework, and his grades were improving. His dad didn't have any reason to punish him. He would criticize the knot in Rom's tie, or tell him he played his music too loud, even though Rom knew he tied a perfect double-windsor and that his father couldn't possibly hear his music from his study on the second floor. Rom would just nod until his father didn't have anything left to say. His dad finally conceded, giving Rom a packet of condoms and a stern eye, saying, "For your girlfriend."

Rom told his father that he didn't have a girlfriend.

"For your boyfriend then," his father replied.

There were days when Rom and Magnolia opened the door and it was too foggy to see, so they would have to go home. Those days, they didn't bother to wander the way they used to, looking for lost objects. Lost objects didn't have the same intrigue as they'd had before they found the in-between place.

Nothing had the same intrigue.

They spent their school days daydreaming about what they would find on the other side of the door. Their conversations continued with the same, effortless streams—but the variety of topics dwindled until they focused on one thing.

The in-between place.

What is it?

How does it work?

Sometimes she would pull out a sharpie and write a quote from a book on a wall, to see if it would stay—but whenever they came back, the place would be different, the words would never be waiting.

It was always changing, sometimes even when they were still there. One time they arrived at an old harbor, stinking of brine. There were rows of docks that stretched into the ocean. As they walked across them, the old wood connected under them like an old dance floor.

There was never anyone else there, but they always wondered who else knew about it. If they were they the only ones.

It didn't matter if they said the same things over and over. They were fascinated by and obsessed with the in-between place. How they found it. What they saw there. They would leave and part ways, practically floating, already itching for the next day.

Summer continues, and they keep jumping over the fence, ducking into the in-between place, wandering around places where they don't belong. They don't belong on the train cars, overgrown with ivy, or walking along the marshes with reeds and dead trees poking out. They don't belong balancing along the train tracks on a tall bridge above a valley, or sitting with their feet dangling over the edge.

They bring books. They bring snacks. They spend hours, talking, or sitting in silence. Magnolia is still a shadow of her former self, but days with Rom are bringing out who she used to be, with quick banter and sudden laughs.

They sprawl on the floor of a forgotten basketball court, the floor crumbling, the lines still painted, their feet in each other's faces. Above them, the sky is shapeless, glowing peach, rose and lavender. He takes off his shirt and lies with his chest facing the sun.

"You should be wearing sunscreen," she tells him.

"Sunscreen has BPAs that cause cancer."

"Radiation from the sun also causes cancer."

"Sunshine also has Vitamin D."

"Vitamin D can't cure cancer."

"You don't know that."

"Well, neither do you."

He sighs and puts his shirt back on. She looks up as he's pulling his shirt over his head and wonders why it's so important to her that he put it back on.

When she's home—which isn't often—she finds herself thinking about Rom. She lies in her new bed and wonders what he is doing, in that big old house that belongs to his father. Does he think about her? Has he been talking to Elyse? Magnolia has found mentioning his girlfriend— even thinking her name—has made her more uncomfortable.

She tries not to think about it, but can't help but ask him, "So, did you come back here?"

They are leaning back, looking up at the sky. They watch the clouds roll along, shifting in patches of color.

"I guess I didn't even realize it was an option," he says. "Like it was off limits, to come here alone."

"Oh—so did you come here with someone else?" She doesn't want to say *Elyse*, not wanting to single her out and make her sound jealous— which she isn't.

"I haven't even mentioned the place—or you—to anyone else," he says. "Why? Did you bring Zane?"

"Oh god no," she says. The thought of bringing someone else there was strange, but thinking of Zane wandering this ever–changing landscape with her felt horrifying. He wouldn't have appreciated it the same way. And she felt like it would have been a betrayal to Rom.

"I would never bring someone else here," he says. "This is our place."

Magnolia returns to her mother's house, latching the gate behind her. The roses intertwined in the fence are shriveled and dark, drooping toward the ground. Just a few days ago they were red and blooming. She touches one of the petals and it's icy.

She hears television static when she enters the house. She can tell the difference now between the buzzing at the in-between place and the static from a television.

She goes upstairs to say hello to her mother.

"Hey—where have you been?" Magnolia's mother asks.

"Out," she says.

"Oh, with anyone in particular?"

"A friend." She's aware of her adolescent one-word answers. She doesn't mean to be evasive or give her mom an attitude. She asks, "What happened to your roses?"

"It's the craziest thing," her mom says. "There've been these freak cold snaps overnight. Killed my damn roses."

Magnolia doesn't say anything.

"Well, my Magnolia seems to be doing better," her mom says and smiles.

Magnolia rolls her eyes at the old term of endearment.

"Oh, I meant to say thank you for the bed," she says. "It's really nice. Thank you."

Her mom turns away from the television to ask, "What bed?"

School was dismissed early because a storm was coming. As they walked, the snow was already starting to fall. It swirled around them as they stood on the platform, waiting for the train. Single snowflakes landed on their coat sleeves, and they marveled at how each had its own pattern—a frozen star—gathered together in a mini constellation.

Their classmates were yelling, attempting to make snowballs, but not enough snow had accumulated yet. Magnolia rolled her eyes.

"Let's just quickly go in," she suggested.

Rom knew that if they stayed too long, they would get in trouble. Their parents would worry, thinking they got lost in the storm. They'd call the police. It'd be a big mess.

But he didn't say no.

They stood on the crowded train, pressed close together. Close enough for Rom to smell the sweet warmth rising from Magnolia's hair. She gripped his shoulder for balance. He caught glimpses of their faint ghost reflections in the black windows, rocking with the sway of the train as it travelled through tunnels.

No one else seemed to notice them.

It was like they weren't even there.

When they left the station the snow was falling harder, faster, and Rom and Magnolia slipped behind the gate unseen.

Snow crunched under their feet as they walked the path to the door. They opened it, welcomed by a blast of frozen air that turned hot as they stepped inside.

The sun was bright and it was easy to forget that it was about to blizzard in the real world. Soon they had to take off their coats and scarves. Magnolia twisted her blue-green hair and fastened it with a barrette from her bag.

There was an empty highway in front of them, flanked by fields and distant trees along the horizon. The road was broken in places, overcome by grass and weeds. They walked and talked like they had before winter. They wandered past a forgotten strip mall, overgrown with vines and concrete crumbling. The storefront windows no longer had glass, and when they peeked through them, they could see sunshine falling where the roof had caved in.

Cars were abandoned in the parking lot, the painted metal sun-bleached and exteriors dented. Tall trees grew where the engines used to be. They walked under the green shadows, noticing how the tree trunks were rusted and dead leaves gathered in back seats.

They walked through these woods and stopped when they found a waterfall. It wasn't too high, and gathered in a deep-looking pool that reflected the perfect blue of the sky.

"We should go in," she said.

"I think that's a bad idea," he said. "We'll get hypothermia or something on our way home."

It didn't matter, she wasn't listening. She was peeling away her clothes and he followed.

How much is she going to take off? he wondered in horror, because he was going to get as undressed as she was, and he didn't want to be naked. Not like this, anyway.

She stripped down to just her underwear, and he did too. She climbed up to the top of the cliff as he was pulling his pants off around his ankles. With his legs freed, he looked up, just in time to see her jump.

As she fell, with arms open like wings and hair floating like sea grass, it occurred to him that they didn't check to see how deep the water was. He held his breath as she hit the water, and waited for her to re-emerge.

She burst through the surface screaming and laughing. She shouted, "Your turn!"

He climbed the cliff—feet resting on mossy rock and hands gripping old tires. He pulled himself to the top, harsh wind licking his face and moving through his hair. He shivered. He walked his toes to the edge and looked down. From below, it had looked like a cliff, maybe two stories tall. But now, it was like he was at the top of a skyscraper. His toes knocked Magnolia's barrette over the edge, and he watched as it fell, disappearing into nothing. He backed away.

"Come on!" Magnolia shouted, her voice carried by the wind.

He looked over the edge again. The pool of water was a tiny puddle below.

"Jump," she said, her voice a whisper in his ear.

He didn't want to, but he did it anyway.

Rom is already at the station when Magnolia arrives. He stands on the overpass, arms resting on the railing. She wonders if this is what it's like, in reverse, when Rom comes and she is already there. If he feels lighter when he sees her, the way she does now.

"Hey." He points toward the park. "Check it out."

The trucks and trailers have arrived, and the crew is out, beginning the setup for the summer festival. Rom's face is bright but Magnolia isn't as excited. The festival means that time is passing, and soon she'll need to figure out what to do next.

"I haven't been in years," she says.

"Me neither."

Magnolia doesn't say anything, and remembers the last time she went to the festival. She'd brought Zane with her, even though he didn't want to. He had brought his friends and they all showed up, high. She was so hurt that she ate cotton candy and smoked cigarettes until she made herself sick. She wonders how it will be different this time.

At the in-between place, they walk along a highway that's crowded with cars stuck in traffic, but all the drivers are gone. Moss covers the hoods and trunks, and weeds gather in the wheel wells. The cars are packed close together, so they can't walk side-by-side. A rusted-open door blocks their path. Rom climbs onto the roof and reaches down to help Magnolia.

Magnolia notices the watch strapped to his wrist.

"Wow," Magnolia says. "That watch is serious business."

"Tell me about it," he says, lifting her up onto the roof of the car. "My dad gave it to me."

She didn't realize he was so strong and has to focus on the conversation again. "I don't think it's your style," she says.

"It's not." He takes it off, fumbling with the strap, his hands suddenly shaking. Magnolia doesn't say anything. She's never seen him so unnerved.

"You should get rid of it."

"Don't you—of all people—think I should keep this? Treasure it forever?"

"No," she says. "Not if it's making you miserable."

He looks over at Magnolia. She looks back at him, not needing an answer.

As he walks home, Rom thinks about the watch. He can't remember putting the it on. And when he saw it strapped to his wrist, he'd felt a sudden chill.

Then there was Magnolia, the look she was giving him as he pulled her up, the intensity in her eyes as they talked about the watch. He wouldn't have been able to recognize it until recently, but there was an undeniable look of attraction. *How could that be?* he wondered. Was he just making it up?

He'd spent so much time reminding himself, *She's just a friend. She's just a friend,* that he dismantled any of the excitement and shine that comes with a crush.

He passes an old car parked in the street leading up the hill to his father's house.

He's surprised to see a car that beat up in this part of the neighborhood. He continues up the street, but shivers again with a familiar feeling of uncomfortable cold. And then he turns back, because it was too strange—and he sees that it's rusted to the point of ruin, and moss has grown like fur across the car.

He closes his eyes, but when he opens them again, the car is still there.

Sunshine creeps across her face and, for once, Magnolia doesn't mind. She stretches across the new bed, welcoming the warm yellow light. She suspects that it would be too early to text Rom, but it's possible that he's already at the gate, waiting for her. She knows his plan is to be out of the house before his dad, and to avoid him at all costs. He doesn't want to be stuck in an office for the rest of his life. A skyscraper sarcophagus. His corner office coffin.

She rubs the last bit of sleep out of her eyes, her gaze landing on a crack in the wall. A delicate line, thin as a strand of hair, has edged its way down the wall from the corner where the wall meets the ceiling. The break looks like lightening in the mural.

Magnolia closes her eyes and starts to think of what books she'd need to review, to see how to repair it, what supplies they have in the house, or if she might need to buy some at the hardware store. She debates whether or not she will fix the mural, or if she will paint a new one. She doesn't see the color draining from the mural.

When she opens her eyes, the walls are white, and the objects on her shelves are gone. She's no longer in her bed, the wood floor is rough and dusty under her. She picks up the pink flower from the floor and a chill runs down her back.

She closes her eyes—feels the warmth of her bed and her blankets—and when she opens them the room is back to normal. The crack in the wall is gone.

She gets dressed and grabs her bag. It doesn't matter if Rom is already there or not. She just doesn't want to stay in her room.

He's standing in front of the mirror, undoing his tie from prom. Except he didn't go to prom. So he knows this is a dream.

When he looks at his reflection, he doesn't see himself. He's Zane, and he just took Magnolia to prom. Except she didn't go to prom.

He would have taken Magnolia, if she hadn't left early for college.

He used to wonder what it would have been like if she had stayed. Maybe the distance between her and Zane would have been enough for her to not go back to him. Maybe they would have been more than friends.

Maybe this moment that he's dreaming would have been real. Maybe they would have gone to prom, even though they thought it was stupid. Maybe they would have had a good time, standing together along the wall. Or maybe they would have even danced.

Maybe they would have come back to his room in the basement. Maybe they would have lost their virginity to each other.

That was a little presumptuous.

She probably wouldn't have been a virgin anymore anyway.

And she wasn't there. He was in the basement, alone.

He juts his chin and works the tie's silky fabric enough to pry his fingers through the knot. Then he pulls to make the gap wider, wide enough for his head to go through.

As he yanks, he notices the feel of the tie snaking behind his collar, pulling tighter.

He tries to loosen and untangle it, but it won't respond. He tries harder, but the tie resists just as hard. He starts to panic, and loses control entirely. The tie slips its way up his neck and starts to choke him.

His limbs start to tingle and his vision dims around the edges. Air stops at the top of his throat and he remembers how when he was little, people would say if you died in your dream, you died in real life.

He remembers he can wake himself up.

He's back in the basement, the bed soaked in sweat. The new basement, where his things from his life before were gone. He stumbles into the bathroom, splashing cold water on his face.

When he looks up in the mirror, he sees rope burns around his neck.

"What if we just stayed here?"

Magnolia casts a sideways glance. "Seriously?"

"Why not? We've never had the chance to see what happens when we just stayed here.

We would always have to leave to go home for dinner or whatever."

"Rom, that would be like—being pioneers in the old west or something. There's no civilization here. Or anything."

She knows it's a crazy idea, but can't help but imagine what it could be like. She was at least a little knowledgeable about home repairs. She might not be able to build an entire house, but if they found a place, she could fix it up.

She mentions this to Rom, and he is encouraged.

"That'd be great. We could live in an old cabin or something."

"Okay." She humors him. "But what would we do for food?"

"We could be like hunters and gatherers."

"Rom—you know there are no animals here."

"I still don't believe that," he says.

"Well, believe it or not, it's true," she says. "We would've seen something by now."

"We could get groceries and come back."

"And I'd have to make a new shelter every time? And how would we buy groceries in the real world if we don't have any money!"

Her voice raises. He laughs.

"Okay, well, one of us could go, and we could peddle something—"

"Weeds? Branches? Bricks?"

"Yes. And then go to the grocery store."

"But who says the place would be the same when you got back?"

"Who says I'm the one going to buy groceries?"

"I already built the house!"

"True." Rom imagines Magnolia, in a house, waiting for him to return. And he thinks of how he would feel if he opened the door and she was gone.

"It'd never work," she says. "Besides, there'd be nothing to do. No one else to talk to. We'd get sick of each other."

"I'd never get sick of you."

Pangs against her ribcage make Magnolia's eyes water. "That's just because we hang out in the in-between place."

"Nah. You're fun all the time, no matter where we are."

She knows that this is just speculation, happy talk, more of their banter. They will leave here today, and come back tomorrow, and nothing will have changed.

They were in a train yard. The engines and cars weren't there, but the ground was covered by rows of tracks. They got tired of stepping over them, so they instinctively started following a single set, balancing along the rails.

Winter had passed, but spring hadn't really arrived yet. Outside, the weather was damp and dreary, but not actually raining. Both just wanted the school year to be over with, but knew that meant they would have to start dealing with applying to college.

They had been coming here long enough to not be so surprised when the tracks began to take new shapes—curving and splitting away so they were no longer parallel, not even tracks, something different entirely.

Trees with thick trunks stood tall, swaddling them with the smell of wet bark. The sky was pale gray and the leaves were bright green. They chatted, following the tracks, and stopped when they reached a tunnel.

"Should we go in?" he suggested.

She looked at him sideways.

"What?"

"No way, dude. Bad idea."

"What? Why?"

"Would it kill you to watch a movie sometime?"

She rarely watched movies anymore. It had been a long time since Zane brought her to the movies. He had said the very same thing that she just said to Rom.

"That shit is so ominous, obviously. You go into that tunnel, you never come out."

"Oh come on—that's crazy."

"Dude! Look where you're standing. A week ago, this was a lake." She shook her head. "Uh–uh. I'm okay with hanging out in here, but I'm not going into that tunnel."

"I'll do it then, and show you. We'll be able to come back."

She shrugged. "Fine, be my guest. It's your mortality."

He approached the tunnel and stood at the edge. He was reminded, suddenly, of how cowardly he had been as a little boy. It didn't help that Magnolia was standing, watching, waiting to see if he was brave or not.

A breeze blew through his hair. Not a chilly breeze, but something about it felt like fingers, lightly tracing themselves down his spine. He backed away.

"Smart man."

"Shut up."

"No, you shut up!"

They backed away and left the place, **and didn't go back in for a while after that.**

They arrive and peek through the door. There's nothing but water. There's no land along the horizon, no distant shoreline. The water reflects the silver sky. Rom bends down to unlace his sneakers.

"We're going to swim?" she asks.

"Sure, why not?" He takes off his shirt. He dips his toes into the water and shivers. He says, "Icy."

"Really?"

"Nah, it's fine."

He stands on the edge, ready to jump, and she backs away, not wanting to get splashed, but also bracing herself to jump in, in case something goes wrong.

He leaps forward, but lands on both feet, barely knee-deep in the water.

"See?" He turns to her. "Come on."

She takes off her boots and ties the laces together, tucking her socks inside and looping the whole bundle through the strap of her bag. She dips her bare toes into the warm water. "I don't know where you think we're gonna go. There's nothing out there."

"There's always nothing out there," he says, holding out his hand.

They wade through the water until the door is just a speck behind them. Then they walk a little farther. They find a dock. It doesn't shift under their weight as they climb on, stretching their legs out in front of them to dry in the sun.

He lies on his back, and she does too. She rests her head against his chest and tells herself that it's okay. It's something that friends could do. Friends could cuddle. They could be the type of friends who did that.

He wasn't expecting that. He looks down at her. He sees the way her hair falls across his torso. He remembers how he used to study her hair from the back of the classroom. He has to tell himself that she is still the same person. Because he sees her now and she could be someone else entirely.

But he doesn't want that to be true.

He touches her hair.

The air becomes harder to breathe. She closes her eyes, and all that's left is the weight of his hand on her hair. Her heart is swollen and she can't tell if it was a residual bruise or if it was inflating with something new.

She reaches her arm across his chest, her hand resting on his arm. His skin is warm and smooth. She can hear the swell of his breath in his chest, rising and falling, louder than the static.

They are the only things living.

They look up at each other.

"I don't want you to forget about me," she tells him.

He doesn't know what to say to convince her that will never happen.

She feels like she's breaking through her eyelids. Everything about them feels heavy and permanent, their legs pressed up against each other. Noses gently knocking. The moment their lips touch, she closes her eyes. But after they part, she's afraid to open them.

She doesn't want to see what will happen next.

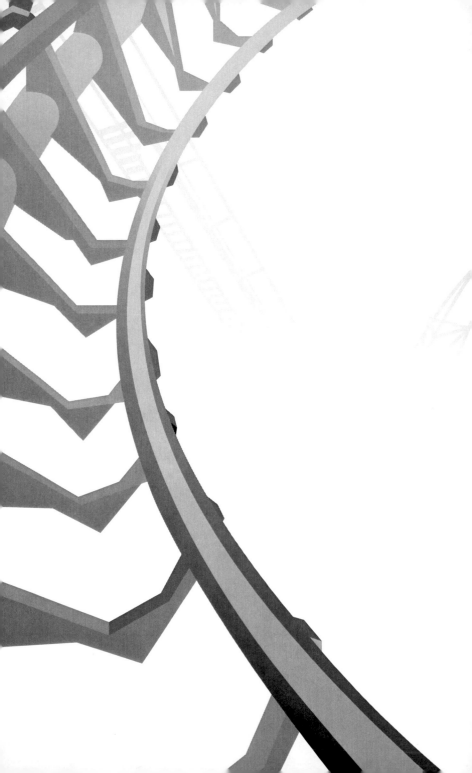

**D**O YOU EVER IMAGINE WHAT TIME looks like?"

"Time?"

"Yeah."

"Like—seconds?"

"Yeah, time, you know, time."

"Why are you laughing at me?"

"Why are you acting so weird about it? T-I-M-E. Time. Do you ever imagine what it looks like?"

"Why would I do that?"

"I don't know—it just dawned on me the other day that when I think of time, it has a shape."

"What?"

"Don't make fun of me!"

"No, no. Explain. I'm intrigued."

"Okay. Close your eyes. Now imagine it's January—what do you see?"

"Snow. And, it's blue. I see, trees."

"Okay! Now—the month keeps going, and it's February—what happens?"

"I see—uh, a calendar."

"What kind of calendar?"

"Like, one of those tear-away kinds that they use in cartoons, that shows the days passing."

"And what's February like?"

"Red."

"Because of Valentine's Day?"

"Probably."

"Okay. So what about March?"

"It's—green."

"Interesting."

"You think so?"

"Yeah. It's different from how I think of time."

"How do you think of time?"

"Close your eyes again? It's more like—a roller coaster."

"A roller coaster?"

"Close your eyes! It's a roller coaster, but it's not fast. And you're not sitting down. You don't even really have a body. It's just the *feeling* of moving in a roller coaster. January starts, and then it moves forward, sort of—I guess toward you? If you were looking at it. And then February goes, like, upward. And March gets higher, but then sort of plateaus."

"Well, what happens next?"

"April and May are at the same level, and sort of, curve around in one direction. But then June starts to go up—and July is even farther up, but then when August comes it starts to dip down. There's a sharp turn at September, and then it plummets all the way down to December."

"Does it start over again at January?"

"Yeah. And so far I've imagined my life the same way."

"What do you mean?"

"Like I was a baby and then really little, so I don't count that so much, but then I start going to school. And I got older. And I can picture the years of my life moving the same way, like a roller coaster."

"Where are you now?"

"On the roller coaster?"

"Yeah."

"I guess, still moving toward the top."

"And what's going to happen next?"

"It has to go back down, right?"

"Not necessarily. A rollercoaster doesn't have to drop. It can do loop-de-loops. Or corkscrews. Hell, they can even change direction entirely."

"Yeah, I guess that's true."

"So, what do you want to happen next?"

"I don't know. I guess I hadn't really thought about it."

SOMETHING WAS GOING TO happen.

Magnolia made a mess of her room trying to find the right outfit and searching through her boxes and tins to match accessories without being too gaudy or obvious. She'd get lost in looking, then would start wondering about Rom, and wishing time would go faster so she could meet up with him sooner, because she wanted to know what was going to happen next.

The last time they were at the in-between place, something had been different. He had this look in his eyes that made her think he wanted to reach out and hold her, and it caught her off guard. She couldn't even recall what they had been talking about, because she suddenly felt self-conscious. She had found a reason to rush home. But once she was alone, her mind had started playing back all their interactions—from their very first conversation—and she realized that this person who she overlooked, who then became her confidant, might be more than just a friend.

She decided that, the next time they saw each other, she would see if he said anything. And if he didn't, she'd ask.

She took one last look in the mirror, pleased with the girl looking back at her. She wore a dress with flowers on it, even though she usually hated to wear anything associated with her name. She actually liked this dress, with its scooped neck and lace lining the bottom of the skirt. She thought it would be too fancy, but her boots defused it.

There was a crash from downstairs, or at least she thought she heard something. She paused, listening, but didn't hear anything more.

Then there was a knock at the front door.

She grabbed her bag, then went downstairs. She opened the door.

Zane was standing on the porch.

He had a black eye and his face was swollen. There were dried scabs around his mouth and stitches lining his forehead.

"Zane—what happened to you?" She was concerned, but she also wanted to get this conversation over with. She knew Rom would be waiting.

Zane started to cry.

She didn't know what to do. They hadn't talked in months, but it felt wrong to just let him stand alone on the porch.

"Come in," she said, opening the door wider. "Tell me what happened."

His face, which had already been patched back together, crumpled and distorted. He sobbed. "I fucked up."

Magnolia had never seen Zane cry before and had to hold herself back from hugging him. "How? What happened?"

Zane told her that he had started dealing. But he wasn't very good at it. He had been selling to some of his friends, and friends of friends. And some other people too, at parties. Last night he had been at a party and everything was good. He had a good buzz going and he was making some money—when some guys showed up, saying that he shouldn't be selling there.

"Who were they?" she asked.

"I don't even know," he said, leaning up against the wall by the stairs. "That's how much of an idiot I am."

She didn't say *I told you so.*

"This is why I needed some space," he said. "I was doing all this stuff and I didn't want you getting involved. So I broke it off. One stupid mistake after the next."

She felt cracked open. She felt herself melt.

"I shouldn't have ever done all this," he said. "I have something for you."

He reached his hand into his pocket and pulled out a locket. They were together when she found it, and she'd never noticed that it was missing.

"Are you asking me back out?" she asked.

"We never officially broke up," he told her, raising an eyebrow.

He asked if he could stay with her. She nodded, thinking of Rom waiting. She felt the back of her neck prickle as she listened to Zane's footsteps behind her, their feet loud on the creaky stairs back up to the attic.

Rom was going to do it. He decided that he would finally tell Magnolia how he felt. He felt like the odds for her reciprocation were good, especially after the last time together at the in-between place. She'd had this look in her eyes that caught him off guard, a look that made him stutter, but also made him feel impulsive.

He kept watching the clock, which only seemed to be moving slower. He started pacing circles around the basement, absently tossing a 12-sided die in the air. The phone started ringing, but he never answered, so he let it ring.

Rom knew there was still a chance that she wouldn't be interested, but he felt that—if they saw each other—he could present a strong argument. She seemed unhappy with Zane, but had a good time when she was with him. He thought that he was nice.

He had it planned in his head. When they got to the gate, he wouldn't hesitate. Just—

Hi.

And tell her.

The phone continued to ring, and he kept pacing, ignoring it, imagining the way she would say, "Thank god—I've been waiting for you to say something!"

And they would embrace.

The exact details in his mind were a bit fuzzy with that part. He didn't want to be so bold as to assume that she would take him by the hand, lead him into the in-between place and take his virginity. Even though that was best-case scenario. Really, a kiss would do. But even that was probably asking too much. They'd probably just be like, yeah, okay. And then hang out like always.

The phone was driving him crazy. Who was calling? Didn't they realize he was about to confess his love to a girl? He answered with a gruff, "What?"

"Rom?" It was her voice on the other end of the line. All his nerves caught up with him, clamoring up his chest and throat like anaphylaxis.

"Magnolia! Hey—what's up?"

"I can't meet you."

"Oh, I was just about to leave—"

He tried to say it like an explanation or an apology, as if saying that would help her change her mind.

"I know, but—something came up."

"Okay—I mean, is everything okay?"

"Yeah, it's fine, I just—I can't meet up today. And I wanted to let you know."

"Okay."

"Sorry."

The next day, her hair was deep purple, and when he saw her after school, Zane had his arm slinked over her shoulders.

She was smoking.

They didn't go back to the place after that.

"**Z**ANE'S DEAD."

He can't believe they finally kissed. His lips still tingle, but her words don't match the feel of her mouth.

"Wait, what?"

She shakes her head, jaw clenched, not speaking.

"Magnolia—please—" He tries to make eye contact with her, but she keeps turning away, refusing to open her eyes. "What happened?"

She doesn't want to see Rom looking at her. What if she made a mistake? What if he never wanted to kiss her? What if she's about to lose him, too? She doesn't want to open her eyes to find out.

"I should have told you," her voice cracks. "I just didn't want to talk about it. I didn't want it to be real anymore. So I didn't tell you."

He doesn't know what to say. He reaches out and touches her hair again. Then wraps his arms around her. She relaxes into his embrace, their cheeks resting on each other's shoulders, but she still isn't convinced that she hasn't ruined everything.

"That's not why I kissed you," she says, "or why I started hanging out with you."

She can feel him nodding.

"I just really was having a good time."

"Me too."

Wind rises off the water, casting a chill around them. Magnolia doesn't move out of his arms, and he doesn't let go. Their skin goosebumps as the temperature drops.

"Why were you with him so long?" Rom doesn't know if it's okay to ask, and pulls away to make sure she's not upset. Her expression is normal again, but he knows that doesn't mean she's okay.

No one had asked her that before, not even herself. That's one of the things she hates. She had never stopped to ask if she was happy while she was following Zane, living a life on his terms, not her own. When Magnolia thinks about every-thing she missed—all the things she could have done, all the ways she could have been—she starts to feel like her skin is peeling off her body.

"I don't know," she tells him. "It just felt like I was doing the right thing."

"Because he was so sick?"

She nods.

"I thought I could help him." Tears are coming and she looks toward the sky to fight them off. "It was stupid. And naïve. I should have known better."

The truth is she loved the way he touched her when he was high. Zane had this way of melting her. And she could really see him, through that drugged haze in his eyes.

She wanted him to see what she saw.

But he never did.

And now she wonders if what she saw was even real.

The water has become too cold for their feet. They draw their legs out, and watch as it freezes around them. The white surface of ice mirrors the dull sky.

"Sometimes I wish that none of it ever happened. That I never showed up at your school."

"Don't wish that," he says.

"Why shouldn't I? If I hadn't been so stupid, then maybe he wouldn't be dead."

"It's not your fault," Rom says.

She looks at him, and he looks back.

His expression is tender. The same look as the warmth in his eyes right before he smiled, when she caught up to him walking along the path after school, or waiting for her at the station. The same look as the sigh after they'd been laughing until their stomachs ached. The same way he brightened when she debated him about some random thing. This look that was warm, a look like sunshine, that she could bask in. A look that Zane never gave her. A look that made her feel like she could be herself.

"I love you."

The words fall out of her mouth before she can stop them, and they hover in the air, lingering on top of the ice. She covers her mouth with her hands before she can say anything more.

Rom smiles, and looks down at his hands.

"Oh my god." Her hands muffle her speech. "I shouldn't have said that."

"No—I'm glad you did."

"Then why didn't you say it back?"

He doesn't answer.

Magnolia can't understand it. She can tell—by his soft gaze and sweet smile, the way he listens and respects her opinion—that Rom loves her.

He *has* to love her.

The way he is—and the way she feels when she was with him, like she could be whoever she wants to be. That is what she has learned love is. She has seen so much, especially coming to the in-between place. Her ideas of what is real or not real have become malleable, but she wants to believe the definition of love has never changed.

"You love me—I know you do—why can't you say it? I know that it's true."

Is it true? Had Zane messed her up so much that she can't tell what love is anymore? Is she confusing love with regular friendship, and just being a normal, nice person?

"I really, really care about you," he says.

"But you used to love me."

"I did." He doesn't even hesitate. "But that was a long time ago. And at a certain point, it was just really obvious that nothing was going to happen, so I had to move on."

"That's so unfair—"

"You can't just love me when it's convenient for you." He isn't shouting, but the words echo against the ice. He's shivering. His breath is like smoke in the cold air. Lips almost blue.

She remembers when she made that phone call, telling him she couldn't meet up. How dispensable it must have made him feel.

"I'm here now," she says, wrapping her arms around him, trying to warm him against the chill. "Please."

At first he doesn't return her embrace. He feels too much like a monster. He doesn't want to hurt her anymore. He hugs her back as an apology.

Rom could hear the bass rumbling as he left his father's house. The music became more distinct as he walked down the hill, the streets getting busier as he approached the park with kids holding balloons, groups of friends clamoring over each other, stepping into the street. Rom was alone, as he had been since school was dismissed for summer.

His friends had welcomed him back into their group, a little curious to know where he had been. He'd shrugged it off, saying, "Just busy after school."

They didn't want to go to the festival, claiming they were too old. Rom didn't care. Hearing the music and seeing the crowd of other festival goers made him excited—a familiar excitement, like the way it was when he was really little, which was a little embarrassing, because he was going to be a senior in the fall.

The smell of grilled onions and BBQ drifted through the air. His stomach growled. He stood by the food stands, deciding between tacos or a pretzel, when a girl at a nearby cart turned and bumped into him.

It was Magnolia.

She was holding a swirled tuft of baby blue and pink cotton candy, and that was the brightest thing about her. Everything else about her appearance was void of color—black jeans with her combat boots, black tank top, her hair a pale lavender. Rom had never run into her outside of school. He'd always been on the lookout for her, for her bright hair. But he'd never seen her, until now.

"Rom—hey." Her eyes went wide, like she had been caught, a trapped animal.

"Hey. How's your summer going?"

"Fine, I guess." She had an iciness to her voice, a distance that he tried to ignore.

"So, wow, I guess—I didn't expect to see you down here, today. It doesn't really seem like your scene."

She shrugged, not offering any more to the conversation. It pained Rom to keep trying, and acting like it didn't bother him.

"Well—I'll let you get back to your friends," he said. "Enjoy your summer."

He turned to walk away, no longer hungry.

"Rom."

"Yeah?"

"I'm not coming back in the fall."

"What do you mean?"

"I did an early application for college. And I got in. So I'm going to finish my high school credits in college. Starting in the fall."

Even though they hadn't talked since before school got out, and this would probably be the last time he saw her for a while—and even though it meant that they really wouldn't make it back to the in-between place, Rom smiled.

"Wow—that's really great!" He meant it, because he wanted Magnolia to be happy. But after she said it, her eyes were wide and wet, like she was about to cry. But she didn't cry.

She told him, "Thanks."

They shut the door behind them. It falls hard against the latch. Their footsteps are heavy as they walk to the gate. They jump the fence and she gives him one last look.

He can tell that she's searching for something in his eyes, something that he wishes he could give her. He says, "I'm sorry."

She nods, and wraps her arms around him, wishing that they could stay. He hugs her back, but she knows that it's time to move on. She can't run away anymore, she has to stop using the in-between place as an escape. And Rom. And Zane. She has to go back and live, on her own.

She lets go of Rom and steps away, forcing herself to not turn back as she crosses the overpass.

Maybe if she hadn't left for college early, or if she hadn't gotten back together with Zane, it could have all been different. Maybe she would be with Rom, now. But would she still be drawn to him, without having lost part of her life to Zane? Maybe Rom wouldn't have been as special to her, if she'd never had someone else to compare him to?

She thinks about how he told her it wasn't her fault. Zane had made his choices, and she had, too. So did Rom. Maybe all this happened for a reason, even if she doesn't like the way it turned out.

Magnolia turns the corner at the police station, and walks up the street toward her mother's house. There isn't any traffic. There aren't any other pedestrians. No cars playing music as they pass by. No police cruisers rushing to a crime scene. The street is silent, except for the buzz of faint static.

Then there's the smell of sulfur, burning more intensely in her nostrils as she gets closer to her mother's house. It gets worse the closer she gets to the house, the buzzing amplifies, and she wants to rush inside, away from the noise and the smell and the feeling of being alone.

She stops.

Zane is standing in front of her house, dressed in a suit, holding a bouquet of dead flowers.

She rushes past the corner, hoping that he didn't see her. She wonders if she's going crazy, or if that was just someone who looked like Zane. She questions herself even though there's no doubt in her mind that it is him.

She turns down the next block, cutting into the alley with looming trees and overgrown bushes. There's a dip in the chain-link fence that she steps over, but it still manages to snag her skin. Blood trickles down her leg.

She steps into her mother's yard. The flowers have fallen and are rotting, petals drooped. Weeds rise between the flowerbeds and grass is growing like the lawn has never been mowed. Magnolia has never seen it like this before, and has to do a double-take. **She knows it's her mother's yard. She stepped over the chain-link fence—and is even still bleeding from it.**

She looks up at her balcony, and can see someone looking out the sliding glass door. Her eyes fix on the blue hair and she gasps.

It's her.

Magnolia can see herself, moving in the attic, and knows that this was the moment that she wishes she could take back.

She enters through the back door, and there's a crash. Her mother's gardening tools had been blocking the door, and the shovels and spades land on the floor with a loud crash of metal. She gently clicks the back door shut, careful not to make any more noise.

She wonders if she should call Rom, but decides against it. She can't keep running to him for help. She could call the police, but how would she explain it to them?

Yes, excuse me, officer. My boyfriend came back from the dead.

She could tell her mother, but would probably spend the rest of her life in an institution. Or if not, her mom would always be thinking that she was crazy and always worrying about her, which was just as bad.

She knows she has to save herself.

She has seen enough zombie movies—it was Zane himself who had sat her down to watch them. She had pretended that they didn't scare her, that she thought they were cool, when in reality she would go home and have nightmares.

All those movies taught her one thing.

She grabs a shovel, then answers the door.

Rom trudges up the hill to his house, cutting through the back woods. The hill is steep and his muscles burn as he climbs, but he wants to feel the ache in his legs. He wants the discomfort to be bigger than the sadness inside him. He wants to forget that look of hurt in Magnolia's eyes, the way she hugged him, how he hoped that she would never let go.

But she did, and she didn't look back.

He wonders if he said the right thing, if he made the right choice, and could kick himself for always being such a coward—running away from his feelings with Elyse, and Magnolia.

He never wanted to hurt anybody.

He wondered if he should just leave. Maybe that would be best. Not to be with Elyse, but to be alone. Maybe that's what he should have done at the start of summer. When Magnolia texted, asking him to go back to the in-between place, he could have said no.

He'll leave right now. Pack a bag and hitch-hike. He'll go to the first place where someone will take him. And maybe he'll stop there, or maybe he'll keep going. He can pawn the watch and use the money to start a life somewhere else.

He crosses the yard to the front of the house, determined to go to his room, shove some things into a bag, and leave.

A speck of cold touches his cheek. He looks up and sees that it's snowing.

Not everywhere. Just in one spot.

The circle of flowers and the bronze statue that was always in the middle of the driveway is gone. The tree is there—the same tree that they had seen the first time they ever went to the in-between place. Except this time, the branches are bare, and where pink petals had once scattered on the ground are drops of blood.

He knows right away that something is wrong, that he needs to find Magnolia.

He turns to run back down the hill, but his dad is standing behind him, blocking the driveway with his black towncar.

"Dad!" He jumps, startled, then gains his composure. "What's going on?"

"No more playing around, son," his father says. "It's time to go to work."

"Okay, but I need to do something first."

"No. No more stalling. No more playing with your girlfriend."

"She's not—"

"It's time to go to work."

Rom wonders if his father can see the strange tree in the driveway, the blood on the ground, the snow falling in summer. "I don't think you understand. This is an emergency—"

"No, I don't think you understand," his dad says. "There's no negotiating."

The car door opens.

"It's time to go."

Magnolia grips the shovel. Her heart pounds hard with adrenaline. She wants to believe that she can trust herself, but she isn't so sure. What if she's still like the girl upstairs? Too ready to sacrifice herself for the people she loved? Does she still love Zane? Did she ever love Zane?

She opens the door.

Zane looks up at her, and Magnolia can tell that he's dead. There's something off about him, like he lacks a certain fluidity in the movement of his eyes. He doesn't take a breath when he speaks.

"Hey, Maggie."

"Magnolia," she says.

He looks confused, like she isn't saying what she's supposed to say. "What?"

"My name is Magnolia."

"Of course," he says. "But I call you Maggie."

"Why are you here?"

"I fucked up."

She hears footsteps upstairs, and knows that Magnolia must be ready to leave to see Rom.

"Come on." She steps onto the porch and shuts the door behind her. She brushes past him and grabs his hand, leading him around the house to the back yard. Light snow had started falling, dusting the dead garden. She wants to tell him, *You're right, you did fuck up*, but it's hard to form the words. Instead she asks, "Why did you come back?"

She hears meekness in her voice, the same vulnerability she always had when she was with him.

"I brought something for you," he says, reaching into his pocket. She knows that he will pull out the locket. The locket she found, and he used. The locket he gave back to her five years ago. The one she threw in the gutter.

She chokes up and tightens her grip on the shovel. She knows that the force of a fast swing will get the job done.

"Magnolia—" He smiles quizzically. "What do you think you're doing?"

She knows that she can't make him disappear, or pretend their relationship never happened. Because then she wouldn't have existed all those years, either. Destroying Zane means destroying part of herself.

He opens his arms to her. "Come here."

She won't be the person she is now.
But maybe that's okay.

The skyscraper stands high above him, the black glass reflecting the overcast sky. Rom follows his father into the building, not wanting to cause a scene. He passes through the revolving door. It's cold inside, a chill that's deeper than a blast of artificial air conditioning. A chill more like winter.

His father doesn't speak as they cross through the lobby, or as they stand together in the elevator, slowly rising into the sky. Rom's stomach lurches and his ears pop. He can't tell if his father is pleased—his face is as stony as always. But he doesn't care if his father is happy or not. He needs to find Magnolia.

The doors open and his father escorts him into the office. Inside, the office has a sweeping view of the city. **In the distance, he can see a swatch of green—the park, and near it, Magnolia's house. He has to get back to her, somehow.**

"You put on this suit." His father points to a garment bag hanging on the back of the door. "And make sure you get the tie right."

Rom's father closes the door and Rom hears a bolt turn. Then the sound of static. He returns to the door and shakes the knob, bangs against the wood. No one responds. The garment bag swings on its hanger.

Through the plastic, he sees a dark navy suit with a crisp, yellow tie.

He strips down and puts it on, thinking maybe they'll let him out if he gives them what they want.

He knocks on the door again, but there's no answer.

He sits at the desk and immediately the phone starts to ring. He answers, "Hello?"

"Rom?" It's Elyse, voice as soft and assuring as ever.

"Hey—hi—can you help? Please? I'm trapped at my father's building."

"I know." Her voice is clearer, no longer coming out of the phone. He looks up and she's sitting on the other side of the desk, smiling sweetly.

"It's good to see you up here," Elyse tells him. "You look good in a suit. You look good behind a desk."

Rom wonders how she is now in front of him, when a moment ago, she was on the phone. The receiver is still in his hand, with faint static tickling his ear. He hangs up, but he can still hear it. "Why do you want me here?"

"Come on, Rom," she says. "It's time to grow up. You can't stay a little kid forever."

"I'm not trying to do that—" he stammers. "I just, I never wanted this."

She looks hurt. "You mean you never wanted me."

"No—that's not, Elyse—"

She starts to cry.

He comes around the desk to hold her. The feel of her body is the same as he remembers.

"You always wanted that other girl."

Rom pauses. He never mentioned Magnolia to Elyse. Hearing her say that, he knows that it's true. "I'm sorry I'm not the person you want me to be. I can't give you what you want. I never could."

Her sobs slow, then stop as the static grows louder. Rom looks around the office, uneasy.

"But you can help me," he says. "You can help me get out of this place."

He feels her nod against his chest. She stands up, her graceful hand taking hold of his wrist, guiding him around the desk.

"Elyse—" he stammers. "What are you doing? What's going on?"

"You know I can't help myself with you," she says, turning his shoulders toward the windows.

"No, Elyse, please—"

"You want my help?" she asks. Then she whispers, "Jump."

The moment the shovel makes contact with his skull, Magnolia knows that she won't have to swing again. The impact reverberates up the long handle and into her arms. And she knows it's done.

She drops the shovels and covers her eyes.

She weeps into her hands—finally crying. She hadn't cried this whole time. Not when the doctors told her that he had died, or when she found her mother at the nurse's station to tell her, not as her mother drove her back to the house. Not any of those hot days in the attic, or when her mother told her she should go to the funeral. Not when she sat on the porch, smoking, knowing they were putting her boyfriend into the ground.

She can't hide from it anymore.

She doesn't want to look. She knows that— even if she does look—she won't believe what she sees. The in-between place has made her question everything so much that nothing is real anymore.

She doesn't want to see his body again. She doesn't want to have been the one to kill him— especially after she'd finally convinced herself that it wasn't her fault. But she knows she has to see for herself.

She opens her eyes.

His body is gone.

Night had fallen while her eyes were closed. The yard is shrouded in darkness, with snow blanketing the weeds and dead flowers. Magnolia is cold. She looks down and sees she's no longer wearing her leggings and sweater, but the floral dress from that afternoon five years ago. She's tired and wants to retreat to her room. She drops the shovel and walks through the house, then up the stairs, to the attic.

Her room is warm, but it's not enough. She wants to burrow into her bed and stay there, maybe forever.

Except there is already someone in her bed.

The body is contorted in the same position as Zane's was when she found him in her old bed. When she'd arrived at their apartment, she'd known something was wrong. It was too quiet. But she didn't know then that he was dead.

Not like now. Now she can tell that this person can't be alive.

She approaches the bed, and notices the floral pattern on the quilt before registering the pristine white shoes on the body's feet. Her mother's feet.

Magnolia backs away from the bed and runs out of the attic, out of the house. She doesn't know if it will help, but she has to go back to the in-between place.

Rom watches the sky as he floats backward. Glass shards like glitter and confetti on New Year's Eve shimmer in the light. Sparkling bits scatter in all directions, suspended like dandelions on a still breeze. Broken pieces chime against each other as they drift toward the ground below.

He watches as the black edge of the top of his father's building stretches longer as he plummets—slowly—down to the earth. The length of the black glass becomes even with the gray sky, and slowly begins to surpass it.

He had always assumed that it wouldn't take very long to fall out of the sky. That he would have hit the pavement much sooner than this.

Maybe he's actually moving just as fast as physics demands. Maybe he's having an out of body experience because he's about to die.

Maybe he isn't about to die at all.

Maybe this is just the world he lives in now.

Maybe now he can do exactly what he wants.

Rom has never been to her house, but he knows where it is. He runs through the park. He runs past their high school, then along the footpaths. Snow stings his face, but he doesn't stop. He runs under the looming elevated tracks, past the row houses, snow gathering on the stairs and windows.

He returns to the station and runs across the overpass, flurries white in the sky above him and in the street below. The snow rings in his ears like electricity.

He races through her neighborhood and finds the blue house with the old porch and snow-covered garden. He rushes inside, calling out for Magnolia.

He flips the lights on in each room as he looks for her. He opens all the doors on the second floor, searching for the stairs to the attic. When he finds them, he runs up the narrow steps, feet slamming into the wood, the stomp of his shoes amplified in the stairwell.

The room is empty.

She'd never told him what it looked like, but he knew that it had to be filled with things she found and made, artifacts from her life. Evidence that she existed.

But there is nothing.

No shelves or books or found photos or collages of receipts and love letters. No music boxes or mint tins of lost jewelry. No posters she bought, no paintings she made. There isn't any furniture, not even a bed. There aren't any walls to cover the slanted ceilings. The slats and pink insulation are exposed.

It's like she never even existed.

He's afraid that she has never existed, and that he doesn't exist either.

There's only one place she could be, right now, if she is real.

He rushes down the stairs and out the front door.

Rom runs toward the station, the fast gusts of snow whip at his face. The sound of a deep bass pounds through the night. He runs past houses wrapped in overgrown vines and the buildings fallen into decay. He approaches the station and sees the park.

It's not empty like it had been when he left his father's building. It's lit with the summer festival—rides moving and contests flashing their lights. Steam rises from food stands but everything smells like sulfur. He rushes past crowds waiting in lines and riding the ferris wheel. They are all punks dressed in business suits.

Rom crosses the overpass and sees Magnolia. She's looking down at the street below, at the festival. The glow of the lights shine violet in her hair. His lungs burn, but he doesn't stop running. He only stops once he's by her side.

She turns to him and he can tell that she had been crying, but there's brightness in her eyes and the hint of a smile on her mouth. There's dirt on her hands and red stains on her dress—a dress. It has flowers on it. And lace.

"You look nice."

She eyes his suit. "So do you."

She reaches up and pulls some glass out of his hair.

"You ready?"

He knew that he would find her here.

Somehow, she knew, too.

It's the only place they have left, the only place they ever had.

The moment they step away from the railing, the ground beneath them begins to shake. The overpass starts to crumble from a distant edge. It deteriorates fast, turning into nothing and coming for them.

They run.

They reach the gate and begin to climb. The iron is so cold it burns, and as they climb, the iron bars stretch taller. They can't jump down and try again because there is no ground below them.

They pull themselves over the top and land on the other side. They run along the path, the ground uneven with snow and sprawling vines. Broken static and roaring trains and cicadas shriek so loud they have to cover their ears. Vines reach out and curl around their ankles each time their feet touch the ground. When they finally reach the wall, they scramble through the ivy looking for the door, the sounds of the carnival, yelling punks and screaming businessmen behind them.

When they find it, it's just a door painted on the wall. They bang their fists against it until the world turns silent.

They turn back, and the path is once again as they always remembered it, summer returned, overgrown and green and quiet. A passing train rumbles along the tracks below.

They turn back again, and the door is no longer a door, not even the painted one.

It's the tunnel.

The smell of sulfur fades, replaced by swells of sweet blossoms. They reach out and grab hands—walking together into the darkness.

SHE OPENS HER EYES.

Sunlight shines into her face through the skylight above her. Half-shielded by the crook of her elbow, she blinks and realizes she is on the floor.

She wonders how she ended up here, in the attic.

The last thing she can remember is coming up the stairs. She was looking at each step as it creaked below her feet. She was wondering if there was a way to make them not creak any-more—knowing that, even if there were a way, she would never get around to fixing them.

Dust floats in the yellow beams of sunlight. She brushes at the dirt on her uniform, but it only smears across the white linen. She sighs and notices that the skylight had made a per-fect square of sun around her. The sun doesn't care what she remembers or forgets. It always does its job.

She stands up, stretching the creaks out of her back and neck. She slips off her shoes and smoothes the wrinkles out of her uniform.

She wonders what she had been looking for.

She looks around the empty attic.

It's rare for her to come up here. There's nothing up here. Just a shoebox with some things inside. She shakes it, its contents rattling, and rests it on an empty shelf.

She opens the sliding glass door to the balcony. The porch's wooden surface is warm under her feet. Cicadas groan and chirp in the distance.

Then there's a blast, a noise like falling metal. Dust rises in sheets, casting a haze across the sky, bleaching the leaves and branches and buildings beyond. The cicadas are quiet for a short while before starting their ascending cry again.

She remembers there had been a notice from the city. They were demolishing the last bit of the old tracks today, making way for something new, different. Maybe better.

She closes her eyes, enjoying the breeze. Then she remembers she has the day off from work. Nothing to do. No one to take care of.

If only she could remember what she came up do. Then, for less than a moment, she gets a glimpse of something in her memory, almost like a distant smell. She tries to hold onto it, to remember, but it's gone. She decides that if it was important, it'll come back to her. She'll spend her day working in the garden.

But for now, she'll stay up here and watch the wind drifting in the summer leaves.

ACKNOWLEDGMENTS

Ever since I was 16 years old, I've wanted to read a book that could be an anime. The book you now hold in your hands is my closest approximation, for now, and is the result of 14 years worth of writing and searching for (but never finding) the book that I had been craving. I have no shortage of gratitude to my editor Tanya Gold and designer Colleen Cole, who told me that this project was possible, and dedicated themselves to making it a reality. These ladies are powerhouses of knowledge and talent and I have learned so much from working with them.

Many, many thanks to beta readers Jessica Critcher, Jude Fils, and Kat Solomon, and to proofreader Ting Hoepfner. They asked all the right questions without once asking if I was crazy. This book was written at the Writers' Room of Boston, or at home with a tiny gray bunny resting his cheek against my arm, and I am grateful for both of their quiet company.

I would not have been able to embark on my writing career without the support of Laurie Myrick and my parents, Dorri and Yao Li. No one was more encouraging of my work than Rayburn and Mum. Except, of course, Kyle.

ABOUT THE AUTHOR

Katie Li writes fiction and narrative non-fiction about personal transformation and unlikely possibilities. Her work has appeared in The Huffington Post, Bitch Flicks, and Xenith. She is a co-organizer of Social Artists and Writers, assistant editor of Novella-T, and curator of the e-zine The Beautiful Worst. *Somewhere In Between* is her first book.